UNTAMED HEARTS

INFINITE TENDERNESS
BOOK 4

MARGAUX FOX

UNTITLED

Stephanie and Ashlyn: The Rodeo

PROLOGUE
STEPHANIE

The second you said "yes," I think part of me knew that you were different. Not because of the way you said it, nor the fact that you said it at all . . . but because of my reaction to it. I'm an organized person, with a plan for every plan, wrapped within another plan. So having every single thought leave my head was a new experience for me.

A date. Where would I take you? What could we do? Where would we go? I felt like all I needed was to be in your company, and then surely the world would spin the other way. But actually, no plan of mine seemed worthy of your time. So I googled, read blogs, and tried to picture our ideal first date. Unfortunately, every scene I imagined seemed to lack what I craved the most: unfiltered, uninterrupted time with you. Simplicity was the only way I could see forward until I had a terrible thought: *what if you didn't feel the same?*

It had been so long since I had even considered letting anyone in in that way.

But you had said, "Yes." Still, I was afraid to really be seen by you. I knew that going with you to the movies, having a drink at the bar, or eating dinner in a crowded room would give me the space to fade into the background. It would offer me a protection that something simpler wouldn't—although being one-on-one would give me unfiltered access to you.

But if I arranged things that way, you would have that much of me as well. *Could I take the rejection?* I wondered. *And yet, could I live without giving myself that chance?* As my fingertips smoothed out the edges of my worn, checkered blanket, I marvelled at the feel of the new, spring grass beneath them. I realized that my heart had decided the answer. Asking so many questions was not the way of the heart, but was instead the result of a planner's mind in overdrive. *What if you couldn't find the place?* I had asked myself. *What if you didn't like the food I'd brought? What if the ice cream melted? What if my skirt split from sitting on the floor? What if it rained? What if we ran out of things to say? What if I was suddenly awkward, or could only whisper? What if you didn't want to kiss me? But what if . . . you did?*

These questions were countered by happy dreams about how things might go. I call those thoughts about you my "wonders." For example, I wondered how you'd smile when you first found me and the picnic I'd set out for you. I wondered how your head might tip when I fed you a strawberry. I wondered how melted ice cream tasted from your fingers and I wondered how you'd touch the split of my skirt—*right up the inside of my thighs?* I wondered how rain on my blushing cheeks would feel. I wondered how I'd breathe in the silence as you looked at me, and how you might smile at my awkwardness. I wondered how you'd smell when you leaned in toward me. And most of all, I wondered how your kiss would feel on my lips.

Questions and wonders became . . . my story of you.

1

STEPHANIE

I sat on the porch of the ranch house, a steaming mug of coffee cradled between my hands. I was enveloped by a profound sense of peace. The air was crisp and cool, carrying the sweet scent of dew-kissed grass and the earthy aroma of the vast Texan countryside that I now called home.

Now, at 56 years old, I finally had my precious morning peace that I had always craved.

Before me lay the expanse of my land, a sprawling sanctuary for my beloved horses. The first light of dawn began to break over the horizon, painting the sky in soft pastel hues of pink and gold. It was a breathtaking sight, one that never failed to stir my soul, and it filled me with that sweet sense of awe. The horses sensed the dawning of a new day and stirred from their slumber in the pastures below.

I watched with a smile as they stretched their powerful limbs and nuzzled one another affectionately, their breath forming wispy clouds in the chilly morning air. Each horse was a magnificent creature in its own right, with a sleek coat that gleamed in the early light and eyes sparkling with intelligence and curiosity.

I took a sip of my coffee and its rich, comforting warmth filled me from the inside out. It was a simple pleasure, this morning ritual of mine, but one that brought me immeasurable joy. With each sip, I felt myself becoming more grounded, more connected to the land and the horses that inhabited it.

From my early-morning spot on the porch, I could see the entire ranch spread out before me. The fields were a patchwork of vibrant greens and golden browns, dotted here and there with clusters of wildflowers that swayed gently in the breeze. In the distance, the rugged silhouette of the barn stood like a silent sentinel, its weathered boards a testament to the passage of time.

The sun rose higher in the sky and its golden

rays began to warm my skin, chasing away the last remnants of the night's chill. It made for a feeling of pure tranquility, being surrounded by the beauty of nature and the gentle presence of the horses. In the soft morning light, I was reminded once again of the deep connection that exists between all living things, and of the profound sense of peace that comes from simply being present in the here and now.

Enveloped in the tranquility of the ranch, I couldn't help but feel a profound sense of gratitude for the ranch- my sanctuary that had become my refuge. The beauty of the sunrise, the gentle presence of the horses, and the comforting familiarity of the land. They all offered solace to my weary soul, soothing the frayed edges of my spirit.

Yet beneath the surface of the peaceful facade, a restlessness stirred within me. Like a dormant ember waiting to ignite. It was a feeling I'd tried to ignore, burying it beneath the comforting routines of ranch life since I had retired from the Army. But as the sun rose higher in the sky, casting its warm glow over the landscape, I found it harder to deny the stirring uneasiness.

I took another sip of coffee, its bitter warmth a stark contrast to the cool morning air. But I still felt my restlessness pressing in on me. An insistent reminder of the thoughts that I had been trying to escape.

I used to have my days filled working as an army doctor. I used to find purpose in helping people. In saving lives. I used to travel the world. I used to serve our country.

And now, only this. The peace of the ranch, the beauty of the expansive landscape and the incredible honor of spending time with my horses.

Captain Stephanie Morley- I barely recognized that name any more.

I glanced out over the pastures, watching as the horses grazed peacefully, oblivious to the turmoil churning within me. They were creatures of instinct, content to live in harmony with the rhythms of nature. As I took my final sip of the morning, I prayed that I would also find my place.

The familiar scent of hay and leather greeted me as I stepped into the stables. The air was filled with the soft sounds of horses shifting in their stalls. It had become a sanctuary of sorts, this place where time seemed to stand still. Normally, it offered some respite from the chaos of the outside world. But today, an undercurrent of tension lingered in the air and a weight seemed to settle on my shoulders like a heavy cloak.

My gaze drifted to Phantom's stall, my 2 year old with racehorse blood in his veins. His father was the great Obsidian Storm.

His dark silhouette standing out against the muted backdrop of the stable. There had always been something about him, something wild and untamed, which called to me in a way that I couldn't quite explain. He was a challenge—a puzzle waiting to be solved. I couldn't help but feel drawn to him, despite the warnings that echoed in the recesses of my mind.

Phantom had been born to a mare of mine always with the intention of becoming a racehorse, but I couldn't tame him. My attempts to ride him, well, they didn't all go well. I had fallen from Phantom many times and I was far from a beginner. I had been lucky so far although my hip still ached from the most recent fall. It was only a matter of time before I got properly hurt.

As I approached his stall, I could feel the tension coiling within me, a sense of unease that gnawed at the edges of my consciousness.

Phantom was a horse of immense potential; of that there was no doubt. However, he was also a creature of untold power and a force to be reckoned with. And as much as I longed to unlock his hidden talents, I couldn't shake the feeling that doing so would unleash something beyond my control.

He was supposed to be a Derby horse like his great father- a winner of the Kentucky Derby at 3 years old. But, the chances of him making that challenge grew increasingly slimmer. In a Derby horse, their 3 year old year is THE year. It is their big moment right there. Then they can retire and live the rest of their life as a champion. Or pursue other horse sports as I always thought Phantom might.

I reached out to stroke his velvety muzzle, the touch of his warm breath against my skin sending a shiver down my spine. His eyes, deep pools of darkness, met mine with a mixture of defiance and curiosity—as if daring me to unlock the secrets that lay hidden within his soul. "Easy, boy," I murmured, my voice barely a whisper in the stillness of the stable. "We'll figure this out together, you and I."

But even as I spoke the words, doubt gnawed at

the edges of my resolve. Phantom was a horse unlike any I had encountered. A creature of wild beauty and untamed spirit. His troubled soul shone like a beacon. Though I longed to help him find his place in the world, I couldn't shake the feeling that doing so would irrevocably change the balance of our fragile existence.

Lost in thought, I barely registered Melody's approach until she was standing beside me, her presence a comforting anchor in the storm of my uncertainty. "Hey, Steph," she greeted, her voice soft with concern. "I've been thinking about Phantom."

I glanced at her, a silent acknowledgment passing between us. Melody had always been able to read me like a book, her intuition a testament to the bond that had formed between us over the years.

"Yeah, he's been acting up more than usual lately," I admitted, my voice tinged with frustration. "I just don't know what to do with him."

Melody studied me for a moment, her gaze searching mine for answers. "Steph, you know as well as I do that Phantom needs more than just love. He needs someone who can handle his spirit. Someone who can train him properly."

I nodded, the weight of her words settling like a heavy burden. "I know," I replied, my voice barely above a whisper. "But I'm not sure I'm ready to bring someone else in. I've always handled the horses myself and I'm not sure I'm ready to let someone else take over."

Melody placed a comforting hand on my arm, her touch grounding me in the present moment. "I understand, Steph. But sometimes, loving them isn't enough. Sometimes, you have to let go to truly help

someone find their purpose."

Her words hung in the air between us, a silent reminder of the choice that lay before me.

Phantom's fate rested in my hands, and I knew that whatever decision I made would shape not only his future, but mine as well. I knew I could send him away to a race track. But, I didn't want that. I didn't want to be separated from him.

As I turned away from Phantom's stall, the weight of indecision heavy upon my shoulders, I couldn't help but wonder if maybe Melody had been right. Perhaps, to truly help Phantom find his purpose, I would have to let go of my fears and insecurities, and trust that he would find his way in the end.

"Steph," Melody began again, her voice gentle yet firm, "I know this is hard for you to accept, but maybe it's time we consider bringing in some outside help." Her words seemed to linger as we stood in the quiet of the stable. A reminder of the difficult choices that lay before me. I knew she was right—that Phantom needed more than just love and care from me alone. But the thought of bringing in an outsider, of acknowledging that I couldn't handle Phantom's challenges on my own, filled me with a sense of unease.

I sighed, the weight of her idea pressing down on me. "I know," I admitted reluctantly, "but the thought of opening up the ranch to a stranger . . . it just feels like admitting defeat."

Melody reached out, placing a reassuring hand on my arm. "It's not defeat, Steph. It's recognizing that we all have our limitations. And sometimes, asking for help is the bravest thing we can do."

Her words struck a chord within me. They felt like truth. But the thought of facing Phantom's challenges head-on, of opening myself up to the judgment of others, still filled me with apprehension.

"Maybe we could go to the State Fair this weekend," Melody suggested tentatively. "There'll be plenty of trainers there and we could see if any of them might be a good fit for Phantom."

I hesitated, the thought of venturing beyond the safety of the ranch sending a shiver down my spine. But deep down, I knew Melody was right. If I wanted what was best for Phantom, I would have to swallow my pride and face the reality of the situation.

As things were, Phantom was a danger to us every day. Something needed to change.

"Okay," I finally conceded, the words tasting bitter on my tongue. "Let's go to the State Fair."

As we made our plans to go, I became more anxious. But beneath my fear and uncertainty, there was also a glimmer of hope—a feeling that perhaps, with the help of an outsider, Phantom could finally find the peace and purpose he so desperately craved. And if that meant opening up the doors of my ranch to someone new, then so be it. For Phantom's sake, I would do whatever it took to help him find his way.

2

ASHLYN

The sun hung like a blazing orb in the vast expanse of the sky, its golden rays casting a fiery glow across the rolling hills. I rode out astride the beautiful bay horse. The wind, a relentless force

of nature, whipped through my hair, sculpting it into a mane that danced in defiance of gravity, mirroring the untamed spirit of the horse beneath me. Every muscle in my body thrummed with anticipation, coiling like a spring ready to be unleashed. With each powerful stride, I could feel the raw energy coursing through the horse's sleek frame, a testament to the strength and discipline that had been instilled in him through countless hours of rigorous training.

I grasped the reins with a firm hand, my fingers tingling with the electric thrill of control. There was a power in the connection between horse and rider—a symbiotic dance of wills that transcended

mere words. Together, we were a force to be reckoned with, a living testament to the indomitable spirit of the wild.

As we thundered across the open fields, the earth trembled beneath us, echoing the beat of hooves against the ground. The world blurred into a kaleidoscope of colors and sounds, a symphony of motion and momentum that pulsed with an almost primal energy. But amid the chaos, there was a sense of clarity, a sharpness of focus that cut through the noise like a blade through silk. With each leap and bound, I felt a surge of power swell within me. A primal roar of triumph that echoed in the depths of my soul.

For I was not merely a rider—I was a warrior, a champion of the untamed wilderness. And in the fierce spirit of the horse beneath me, I saw reflected the strength and beauty of my own untamed

soul. As we slowed to a gentle trot, the horse's flanks heaving with exertion, I reached out to stroke his sleek coat, feeling the strong thrum of his pulse beneath my fingertips. There was a bond between us, forged in the crucible of hardship and resilience. It transcended the boundaries of mere words.

With a final pat on his neck, I turned the horse back toward the stable, a sense of satisfaction settling over me.

As we approached, I noticed the stable owner's wife waiting for me. Her presence was unexpected, but not entirely unwelcome. She stood there, her gaze lingering on me with a hunger that sent a shiver down my spine, her lips curved into a seductive smile that set my pulse racing. "Enjoy your ride?" she purred, her voice dripping with honeyed tones as she stepped closer, her movements fluid and graceful.

I nodded, unable to tear my eyes away from her captivating presence. "Always do," I replied, my voice low and husky with the remnants of adrenaline. Before I could react, she had closed the distance between us, her hand reaching up to brush a lock of hair away from my face with a feather-light touch. And then, before I could comprehend what was happening, her lips were on mine, warm and inviting, sending shockwaves of desire coursing through my body.

For a moment, I was frozen in place, the world spinning as her kiss ignited a fire within me. But then, as if on instinct, I responded, my hands finding their way to her waist as I pulled her closer, losing myself in the intoxicating rush of sensation. But even as I surrendered to the moment, a voice in the back of my mind whispered warnings of danger, reminding me of the complexities and consequences of such forbidden desires. I am Ashlyn Beech- a renowned horse trainer, a woman whose reputation with horses (and sometimes women, too,) preceded her, and any dalliance with the owner's wife could spell disaster for both of us.

Reluctantly, I pulled away, my chest heaving with the effort to regain control of my racing heart.

"We can't," I murmured, my voice barely a whisper, the sunlight fading behind us.

She smiled, a knowing glint in her eyes that sent a thrill of anticipation racing through me. "Can't, or won't?" she teased, her fingers trailing lightly down the curve of my cheek.

I swallowed hard, the conflicting emotions swirling within me like a tempest in the depths of my soul. "Both," I admitted, my voice tinged with regret.

With a sigh, she stepped back, the moment

broken but not forgotten. "Perhaps another time, then," she said, her voice tinged with disappointment. I nodded, a sense of longing tugging at me as I watched her retreat, knowing that our paths would inevitably cross again, but uncertain about what the future might hold.

As I led the horse back into the stables, the echoes of our encounter still lingering in the air, I couldn't help but wonder what might have been. But for now, the rush of the ride and the strength of the horse beneath me were enough to fill the void left in the wake of our fleeting passion. I tended to the needs of the horse while a sense of calm settled over me like a comforting embrace. I knew that whatever challenges lay ahead, I would face them with the same courage and determination that had carried me through so many storms before.

I found myself sitting across from the stable owners wife, Monica in the dimly lit corner of a secluded café, the air thick with tension as I braced myself for the conversation that was long overdue. She sat before me, her gaze smoldering with a mixture of desire and defiance—a potent cocktail that never failed to ignite a spark of apprehension within me.

"Monica," I began, my voice steady, despite the turmoil raging within me. "We need to talk."

She arched an eyebrow, a hint of amusement dancing in her eyes. "Is this about last night?" she asked, her tone laced with sarcasm. "Because if it is, I already told you; I'll be more careful next time."

I shook my head, frustration bubbling to the surface despite my best efforts to keep it at bay. "It's not just about last night, Monica," I replied, my voice tinged with exasperation. "It's about everything. The risks we're taking, the lies we're telling . . . it's not sustainable."

She scoffed, her demeanor shifting from playful to defensive in the blink of an eye. "What are you saying, Ashlyn? That you want to end things?" Her voice cracked with a hint of desperation, a vulnerability that took me by surprise.

Why am I always surprised when they feel differently than I do?

I hesitated, the weight of my words heavy upon my shoulders. "I'm saying that we need to be realistic," I replied, my voice softening with empathy. "We can't keep living like this, always looking over our shoulders. Always afraid of getting caught."

Monica's eyes narrowed, a fire igniting within them that sent a shiver down my spine. "So, what? You're just going to walk away?" she demanded, her voice rising with each word. "After everything we've been through, after all the risks we've taken . . . you're just going to abandon me?"

I reached out, placing a comforting hand on hers, but she jerked away as if my touch burned. "I'm not abandoning you, Monica," I insisted, my heart aching with the pain of my own betrayal. "I'm just . . . I'm tired of living a lie. I need to find some semblance of normalcy, some peace of mind."

She scoffed, a bitter laugh escaping her lips. "Normalcy? Peace of mind?" she repeated, her voice dripping with scorn. "You think you can just walk away from this and pretend like it never happened?"

I closed my eyes, the weight of her words bearing down on me like a heavy burden. "I don't know," I admitted, my voice barely above a whisper. "But we have to try." For a long moment, we sat in silence, the air thick with tension. And then, with a resigned sigh, Monica nodded, a single tear tracing a path down her cheek.

"Fine," she said, her voice barely audible over the din of the café. "If that's what you want, then go. But don't expect me to make it easy for you."

I sat in my small, dimly lit apartment, the weight of the severance letter heavy in my hands. Resignation settled over me as the words on the page blurred before my eyes—a cruel reminder of the fragile nature of my existence in the world of horse training. The terms of the severance were clear. Stark in their simplicity, yet devastating in their implications. I was to receive a generous sum of money—enough to ensure financial security for years to come—but in return, I would be forced to relinquish any ties to Brooks Creek, the place that had become my home and my refuge from the chaos of the outside world.

I screwed up my face. Only myself to blame. Why can I still not keep my hands to myself? Why can I still never resist temptation? Or other people's wives? At my age, I should be over all this shit. I should be settled down with a wife and family, right?

And then there was the non-disclosure agreement, a legal document designed to silence me. To ensure that the secrets of Brooks Creek remained buried forever. It was a bitter pill to swallow and a betrayal of everything I had worked so hard to achieve.

And as I read through the fine print, my heart sank even further. Buried within the legal jargon was a clause that stipulated I could never set foot in the state of Kentucky again, effectively severing any ties I had to the Kentucky world of horse racing and competition. Tears stung my eyes as I realized the full extent of what this meant. I would never again see my beloved horse stallion. Never again feel the rush of adrenaline as we thundered down the track, our hearts pounding in unison with the rhythm of the race.

But even as the realization hit me, I knew that I had no choice but to accept the terms of the severance. Monica Brooks held too much power over me, her influence reaching far beyond the confines of Brooks Creek. To defy her would be to risk everything —my career, my reputation, and my very livelihood.

With a trembling hand, I reached for the pen, my fingers tracing the familiar contours of its surface as I prepared to sign away my future. The ink dried on the page, sealing my fate with a finality that sent a shiver down my spine. I knew that I was saying goodbye, not only to Brooks Creek, to my beloved horses, to Monica Brooks; but to a part of myself that I could never reclaim.

Even so, a spark of defiance flickered within me. A reminder that no matter how far I fell, I would always rise again, stronger and more resilient than before. As I gazed out the window into the night sky, I made a silent vow—to persevere, to endure, and never to let the flames of my passion be extinguished. No matter the cost.

3

STEPHANIE

As Melody and I made our way through yet another state fair, surrounded by bustling crowds and the vibrant atmosphere, I couldn't shake a lingering sense of disappointment. It had been months since we had first attended the fair in search of a trainer for Phantom. But despite our best efforts, I still hadn't found anyone who met my standards.

Melody walked beside me, her expression a mixture of frustration and exhaustion as she glanced at the various booths and exhibits that lined the fairgrounds. She had been my steadfast companion throughout this journey, supporting me every step of the way. Still, I could sense the weariness creeping into her bones—a silent testament to the toll of our fruitless search on both of us.

"Steph, maybe we should take a break," Melody suggested, her voice tinged with concern. "We've been to almost every fair in Texas, and still . . . nothing."

I sighed, the weight of indecision like a leaden weight. "I know," I replied, my voice heavy with resignation. "But I can't shake the feeling that there's someone out there, someone who's perfect for Phantom. I just . . . I haven't found them yet."

Melody nodded, her expression sympathetic, yet a bit impatient. "I understand, Steph. But maybe it's time to lower our expectations a bit. Not every trainer is going to meet your standards, and Phantom deserves a chance to find his potential." I knew she was right, of course. Phantom deserved the best, someone who could help him unlock his true potential and bring out the best in him. But the thought of settling for anything less filled me with a sense of unease. My nagging doubts whispered of compromise and defeat.

But as we wandered through the fairgrounds, the sights and sounds of the bustling crowds washed over us like a tidal wave of energy. I couldn't help but wonder if perhaps Melody was on to something. Maybe it <u>was</u> time to broaden my search—to cast a wider net in the hope of finding someone who could help Phantom become the horse he was meant to be. With a heavy heart, I made a silent vow to myself—to keep searching. To keep fighting for Phantom's future.

As Melody and I wove through the lively atmosphere of the small-town fair, I couldn't help but hear the excited whispers and hushed conversations that seemed to follow us wherever we went.

The air crackled with anticipation and the energy of the crowd was palpable as we made our way through the bustling fairgrounds. Melody, always quick to pick up on the latest gossip, promised to do some digging among the fair staff to see what she could uncover. With a mischievous grin, she disappeared into the throng of people, leaving me to wander the fairgrounds alone, my mind buzzing with curiosity and excitement.

It wasn't long before Melody returned, her eyes shining with excitement as she practically bounced with enthusiasm. "Steph, you'll never believe it!" she exclaimed, barely able to contain herself.

"Ashlyn Beech is rumored to be here!"

My heart skipped a beat at the mention of Ashlyn's name, a surge of adrenaline coursing through my veins at the mere thought of meeting the renowned horse trainer in person. Ashlyn Beech was a legend in the world of horse training, her name synonymous with success- skill and calmness with difficult horses -and there was a touch of mystery about her that only served to enhance her allure. She wasn't like most racing trainers. Sure, she had worked in racing, but she had also worked in the rodeo world. Ashlyn was a cowgirl at heart, her cowboy hat boots and belt that she wore 99% of the time would give that away.

"Are you sure?" I asked, my voice tinged with disbelief. "Here, at this small-town fair?"

Melody nodded eagerly, her excitement infectious as she recounted the rumors she had heard from the fair staff. "It's true, Steph! Apparently, she's been spotted wandering around the stables, checking out the horses, and chatting with the locals. This could be our chance to finally find a trainer for Phantom!"

A surge of hope welled up inside me, though still tempered by apprehension. Meeting Ashlyn Beech was a once-in-a-lifetime opportunity, a chance to learn from one of the best in the business.

But I couldn't shake the worry that gnawed at the edges of my excitement. What if Ashlyn wasn't interested in taking on a new client? What if she didn't see the same potential in Phantom that I did?

I glanced at Melody, whose eyes shone with determination and excitement. And I knew I couldn't let my fears hold me back. This was our chance, our opportunity to finally find a trainer who could help Phantom reach his full potential. And no matter what obstacles lay ahead, I was determined to seize the opportunity with both hands.

We were getting closer to the area where Ashlyn Beech was rumored to be. My heart raced with anticipation and my mind buzzed with a mixture of excitement and nervousness. When I finally caught sight of her towering figure in the crowd, everything else seemed to fade away. She stood out in sharp relief against the bustling backdrop of the fairgrounds.

Ashlyn was about 5'7" and a lean commanding presence, maybe ten years younger than me- I put her at mid 40s. Her long dark hair cascaded in easy waves past her shoulders under her hat, framing her tanned skin and striking green eyes. Her lean muscular frame exuded strength and confidence, every inch of her radiating an aura of power and authority that drew the attention of those around her.

She certainly could have passed for a woman in her 30s, but the way she carried herself and the way her eyes held a wisdom in them let me know she was closer to my own age.

She wore jeans and a plaid shirt and her long legs in tight denim drew my gaze.

Men flocked to her side like moths to a flame, their voices clamoring for her attention as they vied for her favor. Each was eager to impress her with tales of their prized horses. But Ashlyn Beech seemed almost bored by them, her expression cool and composed as she listened to their eager chatter with a detached air of indifference.

Despite the constant stream of men trying to get her to look at them, Ashlyn remained in complete control of the situation. Her presence commanded respect and admiration from all who dared approach her. Ashlyn had an air of confidence about her, a quiet assurance that spoke of years of experience and expertise in the world of horse training.

I watched her from a distance, feeling a sense of awe wash over me, mingled with a tinge of envy at the effortless way she held court. And yet, beneath the facade of strength and confidence, I sensed a vulnerability—a hint of loneliness somewhat like my own. With a deep breath, I gathered my courage and walked toward her, determined to introduce myself and to speak with her about Phantom. And as I drew closer, I couldn't help but wonder about what secrets lay hidden behind those piercing green eyes. What stories of triumph and adversity lay buried within the depths of her soul.

A sense of nervousness washed over me, though I was determined to make a good impression.

Years since retiring from the army and living this reclusive life and I no longer had the confidence I once had. My outfit, a simple yet elegant ensemble with a touch of southern charm, probably showed my Texan upbringing.

"Hi, I'm Stephanie Morley," I said, aware that my voice held a hint of southern drawl. I extended my hand toward Ashlyn. "I couldn't help but notice your presence here at the fair. It's ... uh ... nice to meet you." My words felt clumsy and awkward, a stark contrast to the effortless confidence that seemed to emanate from Ashlyn. But before I could embarrass myself any further, my eyes were drawn to the beautiful sorrel horse standing nearby. He was salivating and looking in discomfort. His head tilted and he was struggling to eat his hay. I suspected issues with his teeth.

Politely pausing the conversation with Ashlyn, I approached the horse's owner, my heart pounding with a mixture of concern and urgency. "Excuse me," I said, my voice steady despite the adrenaline coursing through my veins. "I couldn't help but notice that your horse is showing some signs of discomfort while eating. He looks to me like he is having dental issues- not sure if you are aware, but I just didn't want it to be missed."

The owner's eyes widened in surprise and gratitude, "Oh, thank you so much. I'm new to owning horses, I'll get the veterinarian to check him. Do you know what the issue is?"

"May I?" I asked, indicating the horse's mouth. She nodded her consent and I used my fingers to open the horse's mouth to examine him. I noticed the foul smell and the swelling of the gums around some of the teeth. I saw the excessive salivation.

"I suspect EOTRH," I said, confident in my diagnosis. "Your vet will do a quick surgery to extract the problem teeth, then he will advise you, but you should be easily able to manage the condition in the future."

She smiled and nodded her thanks. As I watched her lead the horse away, a sense of satisfaction washed over me, knowing that I had made a difference in the life of an animal in need. My medic training was never far away, and horses weren't that different to people.

Turning back to Ashlyn, I offered her a sheepish smile, hoping she wouldn't think less of me for my abrupt departure. "Sorry about that," I said, my cheeks flushing with embarrassment. "I just couldn't ignore the signs of distress in that horse. Anyway, it's . . . nice to meet you, Ashlyn."

Now that Ashlyn had seen the interaction between me and the horse's owner, her interest seemed to have deepened, and I couldn't help but notice the shift in her demeanor. Suddenly, she seemed intrigued, her gaze lingering on me with a newfound curiosity.

"So, Stephanie Morley," she began, her voice betraying her interest. "Are you a vet?"

I chuckled softly, a hint of self-deprecation coloring my response. "No, not exactly," I replied, feeling a rush of warmth at the genuine curiosity in Ashlyn's sharp green eyes. "I'm actually a doctor, but horses and humans- they aren't so different, medically at least."

Ashlyn's smile widened at my joke and she was beautiful in the sun under her cowboy hat, and I couldn't help but feel a surge of pride at having elicited such a genuine reaction from her. She seemed to enjoy my sense of humor, which made me feel oddly validated in her presence.

"Well, you certainly seem to know your way around horses," Ashlyn remarked, her admiration clear in her voice. She was charming in her compliment and I liked it.

I shrugged modestly, feeling a flush of embarrassment creeping into my cheeks. "I've always preferred horses to people," I admitted, my gaze drifting back to the horse that had caught my attention earlier. "They just seem to understand me, you know?"

Ashlyn nodded in understanding, her eyes sparkling with a newfound respect. Her gaze lingered on me curiously, but her question still caught me off guard. "It's been a pleasure meeting you, Stephanie Morley. What brings you here?" she inquired, her voice genuine and warm.

Surprise rippled through me at being singled out by Ashlyn Beech. It seemed everyone else was there to ask her questions or vie for her attention, so her interest in me made me feel even more nervous.

But I gathered my composure and mustered a smile, grateful for the opportunity to converse with her.

"Oh, uh, thank you," I stammered slightly, my nerves betraying me despite my efforts to remain composed. "I'm here because . . . well, I own a ranch out east, and I'm looking for a trainer for my horse, Phantom."

As I spoke, I felt a rush of excitement mingled with apprehension. This was my chance to make a good impression on Ashlyn, to show her that I was serious about finding the best possible trainer for Phantom. And though the prospect of speaking to someone as renowned as Ashlyn was daunting, I knew I had to seize the opportunity before it slipped away.

As Ashlyn's expression shifted to one of disappointment at my explanation, I felt a pang of unease wash over me. Had I said something wrong? Was she not interested in helping me find a trainer for Phantom after all?

But before I could dwell on my self-doubt any further, Melody appeared at my side, clearly sensing the tension in the air. With a gentle nudge and a knowing glance, she said, "Why don't you tell Ashlyn a little about Phantom?" her voice filled with encouragement.

I nodded gratefully, seizing the opportunity to share my passion for Phantom with someone who might understand. "Phantom is . . . he's more than just a horse to me," I began, my voice softening with affection as I spoke of my beloved companion. "I rescued him from a difficult situation a few years ago, and ever since then, he's been a constant source of joy and challenge in my life."

As I spoke, I could feel the warmth of Ashlyn's gaze upon me, her interest piqued by my words.

Emboldened by her attention, I continued to paint a picture of Phantom's remarkable spirit and resilience, detailing his journey from a troubled past to the magnificent horse he had become.

"But despite all his strength and beauty, Phantom has always been . . . difficult," I admitted, a note of sadness creeping into my voice. "He's fiercely independent and stubborn, and I've struggled to

train him. To earn his trust and respect as a rider."

Ashlyn listened intently, her expression thoughtful as she absorbed each word I said. I continued to speak of my struggles and insecurities, a sense of vulnerability washing over me. Fear that Ashlyn would judge me for my shortcomings as a horse owner. But to my surprise, Ashlyn's response was one of understanding and empathy. "It sounds like you've been through a lot with Phantom," she remarked, her voice filled with genuine compassion. "But it also sounds like you care deeply for him, and that's what matters most."

Her words struck a chord within me, resonating with the deep love and affection I felt for Phantom. In that moment, I wondered if perhaps Ashlyn saw something in me that I hadn't seen in myself—a strength and resilience born from my unwavering commitment to the horse I loved. As our conversation continued, I found myself opening up to Ashlyn in a way I hadn't with anyone else in a very long time, sharing stories of Phantom's antics and triumphs with a newfound sense of pride. And with each passing moment, I could sense Ashlyn's interest in both me and the horse growing, her curiosity ignited by the bond that Phantom and I had shared and the challenges we had overcome together.

Ashlyn's hand touched my wrist in a gesture of support and I felt electricity sparking through me from her touch. Her eyes were kind and I felt connection with her. I felt my heartbeat quicken. I wanted more from her. More of her.

Something about Ashlyn Beech drew me right in. She was utterly charming and although I suspected I wasn't the only woman she had ever charmed she felt right. For Phantom and for me. She was the one I wanted on our journey with us.

4

ASHLYN

I drove back to my hotel, the events of the day replaying in my mind like a broken record that refused to be ignored. The encounter with Stephanie Morley, the doctor at the fair had left me feeling unsettled. A strange tingle of something I couldn't quite place stirred within me. A feeling I hadn't experienced in months.

In the wake of my leaving Brooks Creek, I had spun myself into a whirlwind of my favorite reckless behaviors, using my money, alcohol, and fleeting connections with women as a temporary distraction from the emptiness that gnawed at my soul. But no matter how many drinks I downed or how many bodies I found solace in, the void inside me remained. It was a gaping chasm that seemed to grow wider with each passing day.

When the girl at the bar had mentioned the fair in Texas, I hadn't given it much thought at the time. But the next day, I found myself behind the wheel, heading toward a destination I hadn't planned. I couldn't shake the feeling that perhaps fate was leading me somewhere unexpected—somewhere I hadn't realized I needed to go.

And then I'd met Stephanie Morley, with her soft southern accent, her golden hair and her gentle demeanor, and something shifted inside me. In her presence, I felt a flicker of something I had long forgotten, a sense of connection and understanding that transcended the superficial encounters I had grown accustomed to.

I drove through the darkened streets, the neon lights of the city flickering past in a blur of color. I couldn't help but wonder what it was about Stephanie Morley that had drawn me in so completely. Was it her passion for her horse, Phantom, or the warmth and sincerity in her eyes when she spoke of him?

Sure, Stephanie was attractive. Older than me, but then we all know I love an older woman. I liked the curve of her breasts under her shirt. I liked the sharp blue of her eyes. Eyes that held a world of secrets, that had lived a thousand lives.

Or was it something deeper, something I couldn't yet name but longed to explore? Whatever it was, I couldn't shake the feeling that Stephanie Morley had stirred up within me, something I had been trying desperately to bury beneath alcohol and meaningless encounters. As I pulled into the parking lot of my hotel, I made a silent vow to unravel the mystery of that tingle I felt in Stephanie's presence. To discover what had awakened within me, after so many months of darkness.

I like to find out more before I take a job. Between the internet and my vast web of contacts I can usually find out a lot. So, I did my best detective work on Stephanie.

Captain Stephanie Morley- US Army.

I found a lot of information while delving into Stephanie's background, but it only served to deepen the mystery around her sudden withdrawal from the spotlight. Her records indicated that Stephanie had been a rising star in the army, her career marked by numerous awards. Not to mention the commendations for her exceptional service as a doctor.

But then, without warning or explanation, everything seemed to change. There were whispers of an incident overseas, something that wasn't documented in the official records but had clearly left its mark on Stephanie in ways that were impossible to ignore. One moment, she was a shining star in the army, destined for greatness, and the next, she had retreated to a secluded ranch in the middle of nowhere in East Texas, far from the prying eyes of the world.

The more I dug, the more questions arose. What had happened to Stephanie overseas? What had caused her to retreat from the world and seek solace in the tranquility of the ranch? And perhaps most importantly, what demons was she wrestling that had made her abandon a life she had worked so hard to build?

Sifting through fragments of information scattered across the internet, I couldn't help but feel a sense of empathy for Stephanie. Whatever had happened overseas, it was clear that she had been deeply affected by it and was still haunted by lingering memories. Finally, I closed the browser window, the weight of what I had uncovered settling over me. Stephanie's journey from army doctor to recluse on a remote ranch was a testament to the human resilience, and a reminder that even the strongest among us are not immune to scars left by the horrors of war.

As I made the call to reserve a hotel near Stephanie's ranch, anticipation coursed through me, mingled with a hint of nervousness at the prospect of meeting her again. It was a bold move, reaching out to someone who seemed content to keep to themselves, but I couldn't shake the feeling that there was more to Stephanie than met the eye. I was determined to uncover the truth.

Leaving a message on the number listed for Stephanie's emergency horse sanctuary, I requested a meeting with her over the next few days, hoping against hope that she would agree to see me. It made me smile to think that Stephanie wasn't listed under her own name or the name of her ranch, but rather as a guardian for horses in need—a silent protector of those who had no voice of their own.

I hung up the phone, knowing that this was the first step on a journey that had the potential to change both of our lives forever. Making my way to the hotel bar to await Stephanie's response, I couldn't help but feel a glimmer of something stirring in me.

Still, I was quick to drown that out with a nice long drink of bourbon.

～

Observing the scene unfolding at Stephanie's ranch from my hidden vantage point, I couldn't help but feel a peace at the tranquil beauty that surrounded me. The sprawling landscape stretched out, bathed in the warm glow of the afternoon sun, while the gentle rustle of the wind through the trees provided a soothing backdrop to the rhythmic movements of the girl who seemed to be a ranch hand and Stephanie as they went about their daily routine.

The two women moved with a practiced ease, their movements graceful and purposeful as they tended to the needs of the horses scattered throughout the paddocks. I watched as they fed, groomed, and tended to each animal with a care that spoke volumes about their deep connection to the creatures under their care.

The horses themselves seemed to exude a sense of calm and contentment, their sleek coats gleaming in the sunlight as they grazed lazily in the fields or nuzzled affectionately against each other. Some were clearly older, their movements slow and steady as they navigated the terrain with a quiet dignity that spoke of a lifetime of wisdom and experience. Others bore the scars of past mistreatment, their wary eyes and cautious movements a haunting reminder of the cruelty they had endured.

But amid the tranquility of the scene, there was one figure that stood out above all others—Phantom. It had to be him from how Stephanie had described him to me. He was a vision of strength and beauty, his powerful frame standing tall and proud against the backdrop of the ranch. His coat, a rich black hue, shimmered in the sunlight, accentuating the powerful muscles that rippled beneath the surface as he moved with a grace and elegance that took my breath away.

A sense of awe washed over me as I watched him, mingled with a newfound sense of purpose. This was a horse unlike any I had encountered, a horse with the potential to become something truly extraordinary. Right then, I knew I had found my reason for

coming to Stephanie's ranch—to unlock the untapped potential hidden within Phantom and, in doing so, perhaps find the sense of purpose and fulfillment that had eluded me for so long.

A sense of determination burning within me, I made a silent vow to myself—to do whatever it took to earn Stephanie's trust and the opportunity to work with Phantom. In him, I saw not only

the chance to prove myself again as a trainer, but also the possibility of redemption. A chance to heal the wounds that had been left when my love of riding had been stripped away from me. I watched Stephanie mount Phantom, feeling excited but a bit nervous about their mismatched power. Phantom's sleek muscles rippled beneath Stephanie's lean denim clad legs as they moved together, his powerful frame poised and ready for action.

But as they began to move, it became clear that something was wrong. Stephanie struggled to control Phantom's powerful strides, her body tense with effort as she fought to rein in his restless energy. And Phantom, sensing her uncertainty, held back—his movements hesitant and uncertain as he tried to accommodate his rider's struggles.

I could see the frustration etched on Stephanie's face as she wrestled with Phantom's unruly strength, her attempts to assert control met with resistance at every turn. Yet despite their struggles, there was a bond between them that was undeniable, one forged through countless hours of hard work and dedication.

I could see Phantom was more patient with her than he might have been with another rider. But, his frustration was also evident.

A sense of admiration washed over me, mingled with a deep longing to intervene and set things right. Phantom was a magnificent creature and I yearned to help him.

The troubled horses, the difficult ones, the ones the other trainers couldn't work with- they were my speciality.

But for now, I could only watch from the sidelines. A silent observer of the struggle between horse and rider, although I could feel the love and determination that flowed between them. Emotion swelled in my chest, as well as a longing to be the one to guide Phantom to greatness. To unlock the hidden depths of his untapped potential and set him on a path to glory.

As Stephanie dismounted from Phantom, exhaustion seemed to wash over her, evident in the way her skin flushed with exertion and her tired body sagged. Her hair, tousled by the wind, framed her face in a wild halo of blonde strands under her hat.

I wanted her. That much was clear. But, I wouldn't let my unruly desires take over this time. I was determined not to cross that line. I kept my eyes on her face, even though they wanted to stray leisurely over her body.

Years of army life had given her an athletic physique that I imagined carried a few more pounds than it had in her army days and I imagined I found her more attractive this way. Her body looked well fit enough for the demands of the ranch, but her breasts were fuller and her hips wider than I expected and I couldn't stop my gaze from drifting over them even though I'd promised myself I wouldn't.

I raised my eyes again.

Despite the weariness etched into every line of her face, there was a determination in Stephanie's eyes that spoke volumes about her strength of character. It was a look that drew me in, capturing

my attention in a way I hadn't anticipated. As I watched her, a sudden wave of desire washed over me, stirring something deep within my chest. I found myself drawn to her in a way I couldn't explain, longing to reach out and touch her, to feel the warmth of her skin beneath my fingertips. Her tiredness only seemed to enhance her allure, adding a vulnerability to her demeanor that made me ache to protect her, to shelter her from the storms that raged within. In that moment, all I wanted was to wrap her in my arms and kiss away the weariness that clung to her like a heavy cloak.

But I held myself back, knowing that now was not the time nor the place for such thoughts.

Again, I felt angry at myself for entertaining such thoughts. How could I allow myself to be so foolish, to let my attraction to her cloud my judgment and make me doubt my resolve? With a steely determination, I made myself a promise—a vow never to entertain the possibility of pursuing Stephanie Morley, no matter how strong the pull of attraction might be. My focus needed to be on Phantom and on restoring my career, nothing else. I couldn't afford to let personal feelings interfere with my goals, not after what happened last time.

Clamping down on the unruly desires that threatened to consume me, I squared my shoulders and steeled myself for the task ahead. I was here to unlock Phantom's true potential and to prove myself as a trainer once more.

I repeated the promise to myself like a mantra,

feeling a sense of resolve settle over me. Becoming grounded in purpose and determination. No matter how much I might be drawn to Stephanie, I would not allow myself to stray from the path I had set for myself. And with that, I pushed aside the tumultuous storm of emotions raging within me, focusing instead on the task at hand. There would be no distractions, no detours from the road I had chosen. For now, all that mattered was Phantom and the journey that lay ahead.

5

STEPHANIE

I felt tired as I dismounted from Phantom, but beneath it, I also felt a keen awareness prickling at the edges of my consciousness. I had sensed Ashlyn Beech's presence from the moment she had arrived at the ranch, her car's reflection catching my eye long before she had even stepped out of the vehicle. You don't spend years in war zones without becoming hyper aware of your surroundings.

Not noticing the details, that is what gets you killed. I always notice the details.

But even though I knew that I was being watched, I refused to let it distract me from the task at hand. Phantom was his own soul, and no amount of scrutiny from an outsider could change that. All I could do was ride him to the best of my ability, honoring the bond we shared and the trust he placed in me as his rider.

I led Phantom back to his stall, unable to shake the feeling of Ashlyn's sharp green eyes on me. Her presence lingered like a shadow at the edge of my consciousness. I pushed the thought aside, focusing instead on the familiar routine of caring for my horses. I felt soothed by the rhythm of their movements.

Deep down, I knew that Ashlyn Beech's presence at the ranch was no mere coincidence. There was something about her, something elusive yet undeniable, that drew her to Phantom and me like a moth to a flame. And while part of me was wary of her intentions, another part couldn't help but feel a spark of curiosity at the prospect of getting to know her better.

But for now, I buried those thoughts beneath the weight of my responsibilities as a caretaker and guardian of these magnificent creatures. Phantom needed me, and I would be damned if I let anything or anyone keep me from fulfilling my duty to him.

∽

Melody and I were finishing up the evening chores at the ranch. Suddenly, she turned to me with a mischievous glint in her eye. "So, Steph, how are you feeling about your meeting with Ashlyn Beech tomorrow?" she asked, her tone casual, yet probing.

I shrugged, trying to appear nonchalant despite the nerves fluttering in my stomach. "Honestly, I'm not sure," I admitted, my voice betraying my uncertainty. "She seems nice enough, but I'm not sure what to expect. I don't trust easily- you know that."

Melody nodded with understanding, a knowing smile playing at the corners of her lips. "Well, she's certainly easy on the eyes," she remarked, her tone teasing. "You can't deny that, Steph."

Heat rushed to my cheeks at her words, and I busied myself with checking the feed bins to hide my embarrassment. "I . . . uh . . . I suppose," I mumbled, unable to meet Melody's gaze.

As if I hadn't noticed.

But Melody wasn't about to let me off the hook that easily. "Come on, Steph," she teased, nudging me playfully with her elbow. "You have to admit, she's totally hot."

I couldn't help but chuckle at Melody's persistence. "Okay, fine," I conceded, a reluctant smile tugging at the corners of my lips. "Ashlyn Beech is very attractive. I'll give you that."

Melody grinned triumphantly, clearly pleased with herself for getting me to admit it. "See, I knew you had a soft spot for Ashlyn," she teased, her tone playful. "Maybe it wouldn't be such a bad thing

for you to get back in the saddle in other ways, if you catch my drift."

I rolled my eyes at Melody's innuendo, but couldn't suppress a small laugh at her antics. "Very funny, Mel," I quipped, shaking my head in mock exasperation. "But let's focus on Phantom for now, okay? We can worry about my love life later."

Melody chuckled, giving me a playful shove. "Fair enough, Steph," she conceded, her tone affectionate. "But just remember, if Ashlyn turns out to be as great as she seems, don't let her slip away."

I smiled at Melody's words, feeling a surge of gratitude for her unwavering support.

"Thanks, Mel," I said softly and with sincerity. "I'll keep that in mind." Hesitantly, I turned to her. "Hey, Mel, um . . . would you want to be there for the meeting with Ashlyn tomorrow?" I asked, my voice tinged with nervousness. "I'm feeling a little . . . well, you know."

Melody smiled gently, placing a reassuring hand on my shoulder. "Steph, you've got this," she said, her tone filled with confidence. "You're the best person to talk to Ashlyn, trust me."

I nodded, grateful for Melody's reassurance, but still a bit apprehensive. "Yeah, I know, but . . . I just feel like I'm better with horses than with people sometimes," I admitted, a hint of self-doubt creeping into my voice.

Melody shook her head, her expression growing more serious. "Don't sell yourself short, Steph," she said firmly. "When it comes to Ashlyn, you're the one person who has always believed in Phantom. You've worked with him day in and day out, and you know him better than anyone else.

You've always believed that he could be something special, maybe even a derby horse someday."

Her words struck a chord within me, reminding me of the deep bond I shared with Phantom and my unwavering faith in his abilities. "You're right, Mel," I said softly, determination settling over me. "And besides, I wouldn't feel comfortable having a male trainer around the ranch long-term anyway."

As if I felt totally comfortable with having a woman I couldn't keep my eyes off around the ranch long term.

Melody nodded in understanding, her gaze unwavering. "Exactly," she said. "And Ashlyn is the best female trainer and jockey to set foot in Texas in a long time. She's the perfect person to help Phantom reach his full potential, and you're the best one to make sure it happens." Her words filled me with a renewed sense of purpose, dispelling the last of my doubts and fears. With Melody's support behind me, I felt ready to face whatever lay ahead, confident in my ability to do right by Phantom and ensure his success. As we headed back to the house to prepare for the meeting with Ashlyn, I couldn't help but feel a sense of excitement building within me, eager to see what the future held for us all.

～

I tossed and turned in bed that night, sleep eluding me. I couldn't shake the nervous anticipation gnawing at my insides. Thoughts of my impending meeting with Ashlyn danced through my mind, taunting me with their persistence. When morning finally arrived, I dragged myself out of bed, exhausted. Catching sight of my reflection in the bathroom mirror, I was frustrated to see the tired, worn-out face staring back at me. Lines had etched themselves into my skin, a stark reminder of the passing years. For a moment, I couldn't help but feel a pang of dissatisfaction at the sight.

But then, I shook myself out of my reverie, chastising myself for such shallow thoughts. This day wasn't about how attractive Ashlyn was, nor how tired I looked by contrast. It was about Phantom and his future. And besides, even if Ashlyn happened to be stunning, just because we were both gay didn't mean she would be interested in me.

My blue eyes once upon a time had been something I had been proud of. My blue eyes had drawn admiration from women and given me confidence in myself. Now, they held none of the sparkle they used to have.

I gave myself a little pep talk, forcing myself to focus on the task at hand. Pushing aside the doubts and insecurities that threatened to derail me. I straightened my shoulders. I was determined to face the day with confidence and poise, regardless of the nerves that churned in the pit of my stomach. With a deep breath, I plastered on a smile and resolved to give it my all, knowing that Phantom's future depended on it.

A wave of gratitude washed over me at the sight of the spread in the kitchen, which Melody had laid out. The aroma of freshly baked goods filled the air, mingling with the rich scent of coffee brewing in the pot. It was a small gesture, but one that spoke volumes about Melody's thoughtfulness and generosity.

I had to smile as I took in the scene before me—the neatly arranged paperwork, the stack of mugs waiting to be filled with steaming coffee, and the array of snacks laid out on the counter. Melody had thought of everything, ensuring that I would have what I needed for the meeting with Ashlyn.

I poured myself a cup of coffee and grabbed a pastry from the plate, reflecting on just how lucky I was to have Melody by my side. She had been with me since the very beginning, showing up on the doorstep of the ranch that first day and asking if I would consider letting her work in exchange for a room.

Facing the daunting prospect of taking on the ranch alone, I had agreed without hesitation. Since then, Melody had become an indispensable part of our team. Her dedication and hard work had helped to turn the ranch into the thriving sanctuary it was now. I was grateful for her unwavering support every single day.

It didn't hurt that the property had three smaller buildings that had always been used as workers' accommodation, which meant that both Melody and I had our own space and freedom. Living on the ranch could be isolating at times, but having our own quarters allowed us to maintain a sense of independence, while still working together toward a common goal.

My thoughts drifted back to the stark contrast between my life in the army barracks and the isolated tranquility of the ranch. It had been a difficult transition, to say the least—a shift from the constant hustle and bustle of military life to the vast expanse of open space and silence that surrounded me now. I remembered how strange it had felt at first, and the overwhelming sense of emptiness that seemed to engulf me during those early days. After spending so many years of my life never being alone, always surrounded by the camaraderie of my fellow soldiers, the sudden solitude of the ranch had been jarring, almost suffocating in its stillness.

But slowly, over time, I had come to appreciate the quiet solitude of the ranch and the sense of safety and peace that it provided. It was a stark contrast to the chaos and uncertainty that had plagued my final days in the army, after the incident that had changed everything.

For a moment, a flicker of that darkness threatened to resurface in my mind, the memories of those final days clawing at the edges of my consciousness. But I quickly pushed them aside, refusing to let them overshadow the gratitude I felt for the life I had now. I glanced around the kitchen, taking in the warmth and coziness of the space, and felt a swell of appreciation for all that I had. Melody was more than just a coworker—she was like family, a constant source of support and companionship.

I heard the confident tap at the door. As I went to answer it, my heart pounded with nervous anticipation. I took a deep breath to steady myself. With determination, I reached out and grasped the doorknob, twisting it and opening the door to reveal the figure standing on the other side.

Even before the door had fully opened, my gaze flew to Ashlyn. She had already stepped back slightly, her attention focused on the sprawling expanse of the ranch before her. Dressed in boots and jeans, she exuded an air of effortless elegance, her form lean and sculpted.

Every muscle was honed to perfection.

The early morning sunlight danced across her tanned skin, casting a golden glow that accentuated the angular lines of her jaw and the curve of her lips. A pair of expensive sunglasses shielded her eyes from the glare, adding a touch of mystery to her already captivating presence.

As I took her in, I couldn't help but feel a pang of awe at Ashlyn's beauty and poise. She looked every inch the seasoned equestrian, her posture confident and assured as she surveyed the ranch with a practiced eye. For a moment, I found myself momentarily transfixed by the sight of her, unable to tear my gaze away from the vision before me. There was something about Ashlyn that was undeniably magnetic, a charisma that seemed to radiate from her every pore.

But then, with a shake of my head, I pushed aside my momentary distraction and focused on the task at hand. With a warm smile, I stepped forward to greet her.

6

ASHLYN

Stephanie Morley opened the door to let me in, but my mind still raced with conflicting thoughts and emotions. Could I really do this? Could I leave behind the bustling movement of Brooks's Creek, with its lively crowds and endless opportunities, for the isolation of this remote ranch in the middle of nowhere?

My doubts gnawed at me, threatening to undermine my resolve. This place was a far cry from the world I was accustomed to—a world filled with people and animals, where every move I made was accompanied by a constant buzz of activity. Here, in this quiet corner of the countryside, the silence was almost deafening, stretching out like an endless expanse of emptiness.

But despite my reservations, I couldn't shake the pull of my curiosity, as well as the excitement that tugged at my heartstrings. The prospect of working with Phantom, of unlocking his true potential, and proving myself as a trainer once more, had given me purpose and determination.

I turned to take in the view of the ranch spread out before me. And then my breath caught at the sight of Stephanie standing on the porch. At that moment, all doubts and uncertainties were swept away, by the sheer beauty of her presence. There was something about Stephanie that was undeniably captivating—a softness to her features, a warmth in her gaze. I was drawn in like a moth to the flame. Her blonde hair framed her face, creating a halo of golden light, and her blue eyes sparkled with a quiet strength that spoke volumes about the depth of her character.

As we walked down to the stable, I made a conscious effort to shake myself out of my reverie and to adopt a more business-like demeanor. This wasn't the time nor place for introspection. I had a job to do, and that job involved learning as much as I could about Phantom and to consider plans for his future.

Stephanie spoke animatedly about Phantom,

her voice filled with warmth and affection as she shared her insights into his temperament and abilities. She answered my questions with ease, her knowledge of the horse evident in the way she spoke. Each word was tinged with deep understanding and respect for the animal.

I listened intently, absorbing every detail Stephanie shared about Phantom's quirks and habits, as well as his likes and dislikes. It was clear that she knew her horse like the back of her hand. I found myself growing more and more impressed with each passing moment.

We had reached the stable and I felt the excitement building within me. I still felt the doubts, though. Could I really do this? Could I leave behind everything I had known and start anew in this unfamiliar environment? I pushed aside the doubts, focusing instead on the task at hand.

As we approached Phantom's stall, I could feel my tension mounting. Stephanie paused in front of it, turning to me with a warm smile. "Ashlyn, I'd like you to meet Phantom," she said, her voice tinged with pride. "He's . . . he's something special."

I returned her smile, feeling a rush of excitement at the prospect of finally meeting the horse I had heard so much about. Stephanie opened the stall door and I stepped inside, my eyes immediately drawn to him.

Phantom was every bit as impressive as I had imagined. His sleek coat gleamed in the dim light of the stable, and his muscles rippled beneath his skin. There was a sense of raw power. But as I approached him, unease washed over me. I had a feeling that something was not quite right.

I reached out a hand to stroke his neck, but Phantom recoiled, his ears flattening against his head as he snorted in disdain. My heart sank at the realization that he was already sizing me up, his instincts telling him that I was a threat.

Undeterred, I tried to regain control of the situation, speaking to him in a soothing tone and trying to establish a sense of trust between us. But Phantom remained obstinate, his gaze fixed on me with an intensity that sent a shiver down my spine.

Stephanie watched from the sidelines, her expression a mix of concern and determination. She had warned me that Phantom could be difficult and it wasn't a total surprise that he reacted to me with such hostility. Despite my best efforts to assert my authority and show him that I was in control, Phantom remained aloof and unresponsive, his mistrust evident in every movement. It was clear that winning him over would be no easy feat, but I was determined to rise to the challenge.

As I assessed the situation, I knew that getting him out into the open would be crucial. The confined space of the stable seemed to exacerbate his sense of unease and resistance. I knew that allowing him some freedom to move would help to alleviate his anxiety.

With that in mind, I made the decision to lead Phantom out of the stable and into the open air.

I approached him, speaking to him in a calm, reassuring tone, hoping to convey a sense of trust and companionship. To my surprise, he seemed to respond to my voice, his demeanor softening ever so.

"Right, I said to Stephanie. Let's get a saddle on and I'll see what he can do. Have Melody saddle another horse and you can come with us."

Stephanie nodded and gestured to the saddle on the wall and let me get on with putting it on Phantom. "He might try and kick you..." she said and although I appreciated the warning, I didn't need it. I knew he was unsure and I knew there was always that risk with a horse like him.

"Mel, can you saddle Snow for me? I'll take him out with Phantom and Ashlyn."

I positioned my body at all times to avoid his back legs should he choose to strike.

He didn't kick out at me and I was pleased with that. It was a good start.

I lead him out of the barn and into the open air and positioned myself by his saddle on his left side. I looked to Stephanie and raised my right foot asking without words in a language that all horse people understood- I was asking for her to hold my leg and boost me up onto the horse.

She moved towards me and as soon as I felt the touch of her hands on my shin, I felt a jolt of connection with her. I wanted her hands to run up my leg much further than where they were at my shin. There was something between us and I couldn't shake it.

I hopped and she boosted me and within seconds I swung my right leg over and was astride Phantom.

This was my happy place. Riding was as natural to me as walking. I couldn't remember a time before I could ride.

I sat quietly, allowing Phantom to figure things out himself as Stephanie mounted a smaller white horse and came to join us.

We began to move, and I could feel Phantom's

muscles tense beneath me, his movements hesitant and uncertain. But with each stride, I worked to assert my control, guiding him with firm yet gentle cues from my legs and ass.

We set off, anticipation crackling in the air like electricity, the tension palpable between Phantom and me and well, Stephanie and me. Obviously I was focussed on the horse.. but...

Things started well, Stephanie and I rode and talked and things felt easy. There was an easy peace between us that I liked. I think Phantom liked it too as he almost felt relaxed at times.

We approached a sand track that was clear it was used to run the horses and I felt Phantom becoming tense beneath me. He knew this was where they liked to run. Meanwhile Stephanie's white horse broke into a jog beneath her and I admired her calm hands and the lovely line of her body as it became one with the horse beneath her.

Oh, to be between those thighs.

"We won't run them today," I said. "I know horses are creatures of habit and they won't like it but he mostly needs to learn to relax."

Stephanie nodded.

I could sense Phantom's anger as I turned him

past the entrance to his track and asked him just to walk for me, his muscles coiled like springs beneath me. I sat quietly. His movements became jerky and erratic as he tried to throw me off balance. I sat calmly again. The worst thing you can do with a tense horse is to transmit tension yourself or to let yourself show any fear. Phantom suddenly launched and began to buck and twist beneath me as though he no longer wanted a rider along for the journey. Each jolt sent a shockwave of adrenaline coursing through my veins and I used my core and my balance learnt from riding a thousand horses like this to stay in the saddle and stay calm.

I rode out the storm and kept asking as calmly as I could for walk and for relaxation and eventually, realising I wasn't going anywhere and I wasn't actually forcing him to do anything, he calmed and I felt him relax beneath me.

A small win.

It was a start.

I met Stephanie's eyes as she smiled at me. "I knew you were the right one for him. I could sense it. Not many riders would still be sitting aboard right now, you were incredible,"

I knew that was true. Being able to stay on a

difficult horse when it decides it doesn't want you there is half the battle.

"Ah, it was easy," I gave my best charming smile back knowing full well the effect it had on women.

I watched as Stephanie's blue eyes looked away and a flush ran through her cheeks.

Seeing a beautiful woman flustered by me was something I was a big fan of.

Stop it, Ashlyn. For god's sake.

We made it back to the barn in one piece and we dismounted. As I stood beside Phantom, his eyes searched mine for some sign of weakness. But then, in a fleeting moment of unexpected tenderness, he nuzzled my hand, as though a silent acknowledgment of our shared struggle.

We both returned our horses to their stalls and stripped them of the saddle and bridles they were wearing. As I removed Phantom's saddle pad the steam rose from his body.

I left the stall and turned to face Stephanie. I could see the kaleidoscope of emotions flickering across her face— awe, uncertainty, and something else. Something I couldn't quite name. Her blue eyes were fixed on mine. Her lips were parted.

Without a second thought, I closed the distance between us. My hand reached out to cup her cheek as I leaned in to press my lips against hers. The kiss was gentle yet passionate, a silent confession of the emotions swirling between us. A moment of vulnerability and connection amid the chaos of the morning.

Time seemed to stand still as our lips met, the world falling away as we lost ourselves in the heat of it. Her mouth opened and my tongue pushed inside.

And in that brief, stolen moment, I felt a sense of clarity wash over me—a realization that despite the challenges we faced, despite my uncertainty about the future, there was something undeniable between us.

But as quickly as it had begun, the moment was over. I pulled back, my heart pounding with exhilaration and trepidation. Stephanie's eyes met mine, wide with surprise and uncertainty. For a moment, neither of us spoke, the weight of what we had done hanging heavy in the air. Then, with a shaky breath, Stephanie reached out to touch my cheek, sending a shiver down my spine. "Ashlyn," she whispered, her voice barely above a whisper, "what was that?"

I searched her eyes, looking for some sign of understanding, some indication of what had just passed between us. But I found uncertainty and a flicker of fear dancing in the depths of her gaze.

"I don't know," I admitted, my voice barely a whisper. "But... but I couldn't help myself. There's something about you, Stephanie. Something that draws me to you like a moth to a flame."

Stephanie's expression softened, a hint of warmth flickering in her eyes as she reached out to take my hand in hers. "I feel it too, Ashlyn," she said, her voice barely above a whisper. "There's something between us, something... undeniable."

I knew this wasn't the first time I had done something like this and I didn't want to put this on Stephanie, too.

I couldn't shake the memory of what had happened with Monica—the risks, the consequences, and the heartache. Despite the undeniable connection I felt with Stephanie, I knew I couldn't afford to let my guard down again. Couldn't risk opening myself up to the possibility of getting hurt. And, in turn, hurting her.

With a heavy heart, I pulled away from Stephanie, my gaze dropping to the ground as I struggled to find the words to explain.

So, I didn't.

"I... I would like to take the job, if it's still

available," I said, my voice curt and businesslike. "I'll be back tomorrow to go through the paperwork." I could feel Stephanie's eyes on me, trying to understand what had changed between us. But I couldn't bring myself to meet her gaze. I couldn't bear to see the hurt and confusion in her eyes.

For a moment, there was silence between us, the weight of our unspoken emotions hanging heavy in the air. And then, with a nod of resignation, Stephanie spoke, her voice tinged with a hint of sadness. "Of course," she said, her tone subdued. "I'll have everything ready for you tomorrow."

I turned to leave, but couldn't shake the sense of regret that gnawed at my insides. The knowledge that I had hurt Stephanie with my sudden change in demeanor. But I knew it was for the best. I couldn't afford to let my emotions cloud my judgment—not when so much was at stake. With a heavy heart, I walked away, leaving Stephanie behind in the quiet solitude of the ranch.

7

STEPHANIE

I kept up my work on the ranch that day, but my mind relived the unexpected kiss I had shared with Ashlyn. The memory was like a flickering flame, dancing at the edges of my consciousness.

It refused to be extinguished, despite my best effort to focus on the tasks at hand. I knew I should be thinking about Phantom and about how well he had responded to Ashlyn as a rider.

About the progress they made together.

Instead, all I could remember was how Ashlyn's lips had felt against mine—soft and warm. How it had felt when her tongue pressed into my mouth. Oh, I wanted that again, and so much more. A fleeting moment of intimacy had

Untamed Hearts

left me breathless and wanting more. With a sigh, I shook my head, trying to banish the memory from my mind. This was no time for daydreams and distractions, not when there was so much work to be done on the ranch.

But try as I might, I couldn't shake the feeling of longing that tugged at my heartstrings, my desire to be near Ashlyn once more. To feel her touch and to taste her kiss. As I tended to the horses, my movements were mechanical, my thoughts consumed by the memory of our stolen moment of passion. I could feel a blush creeping into my cheeks as I replayed the kiss in my mind, each sensation seared into my memory with crystal clarity.

But amid the swirl of emotions that threatened to overwhelm me, there was a small voice of reason, reminding me of the risks of getting involved with Ashlyn. I knew the dangers all too well—the potential for heartache, for betrayal, for loss. And yet I couldn't deny the pull of attraction that drew me to her.

I wondered for a second if I was just one of many. If that was the effect she had on women. I had known women like her before, in the army. Of course I had. We all know a lesbian like her. Effortlessly charming. Strikingly beautiful, with a smile that melts hearts. All the women want her, of course they do. And she wants (and takes) all of them. Then she leaves a trail of broken hearts behind her.

I certainly did not want to be one of a trail of broken hearts, that was for sure.

Yet, here was someone who excited me in a way that I hadn't felt in so many years. Would it be so wrong to pursue that?

With a shake of my head, I forced myself to focus on the present, pushing aside the lingering thoughts of Ashlyn's kiss. There would be time enough for contemplation later, time enough to unravel the mysteries of my heart. But for now, there were horses to tend to, chores to be done, and a ranch to run.

I made my way up to the house, my thoughts still swirling with memories of our kiss, finding myself faced with the practical realities. Melody was waiting for me in the kitchen, a stack of paperwork spread out on the table before her.

"Hey, Steph," she greeted me with a warm smile. "I've got everything ready for Ashlyn's paperwork."

I nodded, taking a seat opposite her as she

began to explain the details of the arrangement we had agreed upon for Ashlyn's employment. As Melody spoke, I couldn't help but feel a pang of unease at the thought of bringing someone new onto the ranch, especially someone as enigmatic and unpredictable as Ashlyn.

But despite my reservations, I knew that Ashlyn's expertise could be just what Phantom needed. And if it meant putting aside my own misgivings for the sake of the horse, then I was willing to do whatever it took.

As Melody outlined the terms of Ashlyn's employment, I couldn't help but notice the absence of any references or paperwork from Ashlyn herself. It seemed strange, given the importance of such

documentation in a professional setting. However, I pushed aside my concerns, trusting my gut instinct that Ashlyn was the right choice for the job.

Phantom had kicked off in the way he was so prone to when things didn't go exactly his way. His whole body had twisted as he bucked and leapt and I knew for a fact had it been me in his saddle at that time he would have thrown me off again. I was far too old for falling off horses. My right hip still ached with the memory of last time. But the way Ashlyn had been on him, her beautiful athletic body sitting easily aboard him, moving with him, adjusting her balance constantly to stay in motion with him. She was a calm and quiet rider- there was no harsh discipline for Phantom, just a quiet welcome for him when he calmed down and Ashlyn was still there- completely unphased. Her face looked just as calm as ever and that passed down to the horse. Horses sense things in people. Phantom especially.

"Everything looks good," I said, forcing a smile as I signed my name on the dotted line. "Let's hope Ashlyn feels the same way."

Melody nodded, her brow furrowed with worry. "I'm just not sure about the pay, Steph," she admitted, her voice tinged with concern. "It's not much, and Ashlyn might not be willing to accept it."

I sighed, knowing that she was right. The salary we were offering was far from generous, especially given Ashlyn's reputation as a renowned horse trainer. But it was the best I could afford. I sensed that Ashlyn had her reasons for wanting to move out here and I figured money wasn't the motivator.

"We'll just have to wait and see," I said with a shrug, trying to sound more confident than I felt. "If Ashlyn is as passionate about horses as she seems, then hopefully she'll understand that this is about more than just money."

∽

I stirred from sleep, my heart still racing from the vivid dream that had consumed me. I found that I was bathed in a sheen of sweat, my breath coming in shallow gasps. The memory of Ashlyn's kiss lingered on my lips, and the sensation still tingled against my skin as if it had been real.

I sat up in bed, disoriented and flustered, trying to shake off the remnants of the dream that had felt so achingly real. In the darkness of my room, I could still feel the warmth of Ashlyn's touch, the weight of her lips against mine, and I couldn't help the surge of longing that rose up within my chest.

But once the fog of sleep began to lift, reality came crashing back down upon me. It was a harsh reminder of the boundaries that existed between us. I knew that what I had imagined in my dream could never be—a fleeting moment of passion, a stolen kiss in the darkness of night.

With a sigh, I pushed aside the tangled sheets and swung my legs over the edge of the bed, the cool air of the room washing over me like a balm. I knew that dwelling on my dreams would only lead to trouble.

With a shake of my head, I forced myself to focus on the present, pushing aside the fantasies that danced at the edges of my consciousness. There would be time enough for contemplation later,

time enough to unravel the mysteries of my heart. But for now, I had a ranch to run.

I stumbled into the kitchen, my mind still reeling from the remnants of my interrupted dream. I was surprised to find Ashlyn already there, seated at the table alongside Melody, signing paperwork. Seeing Ashlyn sent a jolt of surprise through me and my heart skipped a beat at the unexpected encounter. I hadn't expected to encounter her so early in the morning, especially not after the previous day's events.

"Good morning," Ashlyn said, greeting me with a warm smile. Her gaze met mine and a hint of amusement danced in her eyes. "I hope you don't mind, but Melody and I thought we'd get a head start on the paperwork."

I blinked in confusion, still trying to process the sight before me. It was clear that Ashlyn had accepted the job offer, despite the low pay and the uncertainty of our arrangement. And yet, there was something in her demeanor that seemed different, a sense of determination and resolve that I hadn't seen before.

"Of course I don't mind," I replied, my voice tinged with surprise. "I'm just . . . I'm surprised to see you here so early."

Ashlyn shrugged, her expression casual yet determined. "I wanted to get started right away," she explained, her tone firm. "I'm eager to get to work with Phantom and see what we can accomplish together."

I nodded, unable to hide the sense of relief that washed over me at her words. Despite my reservations and despite the risks, I couldn't help but feel a surge of excitement at the prospect of working with Ashlyn.

As we gathered around the table, Ashlyn wasted no time in diving into her plan for Phantom. Her demeanor was focused and her tone confident as she outlined her observations and the strategies she wanted to try.

"So, here's what I've noticed," she began, her voice firm yet measured. "Phantom is a strong, powerful horse with a lot of potential. But he's also highly sensitive, stubborn and resistant to authority, which is why he's been so difficult to train."

I nodded, acknowledging the truth in her words. Phantom had always been a challenge, his rebellious spirit proving to be a formidable obstacle.

"But I believe that with the right approach, we can make some real progress," Ashlyn continued, her gaze steady as she met my eyes. Her green eyes were intense.

"First and foremost, we need to establish trust and respect between us and Phantom. Without that foundation, any attempts at training will be doomed to fail."

I listened intently as Ashlyn outlined her plan, her words painting a vivid picture of the challenges that lay ahead and the strategies she proposed to overcome them.

"We'll start by working on ground manners," she explained, her voice firm. "Phantom needs to learn to be calm around us on the ground. That means reinforcing basic commands like 'halt,' 'back up,' and 'stand.' We don't want anyone going in his stall and being at risk of being kicked."

I nodded in agreement, recognizing the importance of establishing clear boundaries and expectations with Phantom before attempting to tackle more advanced training techniques.

"Once we've established trust and respect on the ground, we can start re-introducing him to the saddle," Ashlyn continued, her tone confident. "But it's important to take things slow and steady, he needs to be calm and willing at each stage. It is pointless starting a war with him every time we get on him. Pointless having to try and cling on each time when he starts his antics. If he carries on like this, someone will get seriously hurt."

I listened intently as Ashlyn outlined her plan, her words filled with wisdom and the experience gained from years of working with difficult horses. It was clear that she was passionate about her craft.

"And of course, we'll need to address any underlying physical issues that may be contributing to Phantom's behavior," Ashlyn added, her voice tinged with concern. "I'll need to conduct a thorough examination to rule out any pain or discomfort that may be causing him to act out." I nodded in agreement, but also felt confident she would find no physical ailments. Phantom's problems were all in his mind- I was confident of that.

"Let's start with his daily schedule," she began, her voice firm and authoritative. "I need to know exactly what Phantom's routine looks like, from the moment he wakes up to the moment he goes to bed.

Consistency is key when it comes to training, and I want to make sure we're providing Phantom with the structure and stability he needs to thrive."

I nodded in agreement, recognizing the importance of establishing a consistent routine for Phantom to follow. His schedule had always been somewhat haphazard, with tasks and chores often taking precedence over any kind of routine for the horses.

On another level, my body was reacting to Ashlyn's presence. I couldn't help but feel a flush run through me when I heard her speak in such an authoritarian manner. Maybe because I was so used to military direction, or else my own slightly submissive nature when it came to intimacy, I found that her words and the intensity of her green eyes sent heat right through me like a lightning bolt.

"Next, I'll need to know about his diet," Ashlyn continued, her tone serious. "What does he eat? How much, and how often? Proper nutrition is essential for maintaining his health and energy levels,

but being careful not to feed foods that will make him too buzzed."

I rattled off the details of Phantom's diet, from the type of hay he preferred to his favorite treats and supplements. It helped to get my mind back on track.

Sort of.

Because there in front of me, temptingly close was Ashlyn Beech. Her full lips- the ones that kissed me- taunting me.

I wanted her to kiss me again.

I wanted to hear that direct authoritative tone of her voice in the bedroom.

Heat flooded between my legs.

It was going to be one hell of a challenge to remain professional around her.

8

ASHLYN

I watched Stephanie's reactions to my directives regarding Phantom, and I couldn't help but notice the subtle shifts in her body language. My ability to read body language had been honed over years of working with horses, allowing me to understand their needs and responses with remarkable precision. Yet it was the human nuances that often proved the most intriguing.

My ability to read women was a close second to my ability to read horses.

Stephanie's initial response to my authoritative tone surprised me. I had expected her to meet my direction with a more assertive demeanor, given her history, her age and her role. But as I watched her more closely, I couldn't help but notice the telltale signs of discomfort that belied her outward confidence. There was tension in Stephanie's shoulders and a slight stiffness in her posture that betrayed her unease with my assertiveness. Her blue eyes, normally steady and unwavering, flickered with uncertainty as they met mine, a subtle indication of her internal struggle.

In that moment, realization dawned on me—an understanding that went beyond our discussion of Phantom's training. It was clear that Stephanie's response wasn't simply about her desire to maintain control over the ranch. There was something more beneath the surface, something that spoke to a deeper connection between us.

As I continued to watch Stephanie, curiosity mingled with my newfound awareness of her. I couldn't help but wonder what lay behind this beautiful woman's guarded façade. What emotions were

churning beneath the surface. And then it struck me—a realization so unexpected that it took my breath away. Stephanie's response wasn't rooted in defiance or resistance, but rather in something far more complex—a blend of attraction and vulnerability that she was trying to hide from me.

In that moment, I understood the unspoken truth that lingered between us. Undeniable chemistry crackled in the air whenever our paths crossed. And as I met Stephanie's gaze, a silent acknowledgment passed between us. Both of us recognized the unspoken desires that pulsed beneath the surface.

With a silent vow to tread carefully, I returned my attention to the matter at hand, determined to navigate the complexities of our relationship with caution and care. But deep down, I knew that the

bond between us was stronger than mere words could convey—a bond forged in the fires of passion.

My mind drifted back to the journey that had brought me to this moment. A journey marked by moments of self-discovery and introspection. The trials and triumphs that had shaped the woman I had become. I had always known, on some level, that I was different—that my desires and attractions diverged from the conventional norms society prescribed. Yet, it wasn't until my late teens that I fully

embraced my truth, acknowledging and

accepting my sexuality as a fundamental aspect of my core being. I was unapologetic and unashamed.

During the years that followed, I embarked on a journey of exploration, seeking to understand the depths of my desires and the intricacies of my sexuality. There had been nights of experimentation, nights of passion and pleasure shared with partners who had come and gone, each leaving their mark on

me in their own unique way. But through it all, one truth had remained constant—an unwavering certainty that I liked to be dominant, both in and out of the bedroom. While some reveled in the thrill of switching roles, embracing the fluidity of their desires, I found solace in the unyielding strength of my dominance.

It was a force that defined me in ways I couldn't fully articulate. It wasn't just about physical control or power dynamics; it was about a deeper connection—a sense of purpose and fulfillment that transcended the physical realm. It was about embracing my true self, unapologetically and unabashedly, and finding someone who could meet me on that level.

As my thoughts swirled with the complexities

of my feelings for Stephanie, I couldn't help but notice Melody's gaze lingering on us. Her eyes darted back and forth between Stephanie and me, a curious expression flickering across her features. For a brief moment, I felt a surge of panic rise within me, wondering if Melody had somehow sensed the tension that crackled in the air.

But as I studied Melody's expression more closely, I realized that her gaze held more curiosity than suspicion. There was a knowing glint in her eyes, a silent acknowledgment of the unspoken connection that simmered between Stephanie and me. It was clear that Melody was attuned to the subtle nuances of our interactions. To the unspoken gestures and shared glances that spoke volumes about the bond we shared. And while Melody's gaze held a hint of curiosity, there was also a sense of understanding. A silent acceptance of the situation's complexities.

∼

I walked down to the ranch with Phantom by my side. As I approached the stables, I caught sight of Stephanie returning from her ride with Kenco, a seasoned horse who had been a part of the ranch for years. The two of them moved together with an effortless grace, their movements synchronized in perfect harmony.

Stephanie looked radiant, her eyes sparkling with joy as she dismounted from Kenco's back. There was a sense of fulfillment in her demeanor, a quiet confidence that spoke volumes about the bond

she shared with him. "Ashlyn," Stephanie greeted me. She smiled warmly, her voice filled with happiness.

"Looks like you and Phantom are getting along just fine."

I returned her smile, feeling a sense of camaraderie wash over me. "He's a remarkable horse," I replied. "And you and Kenco make quite the pair as well."

I couldn't help my gaze running over the shape of the thighs in tight denim.

Stephanie's smile widened at my words, a sense of pride evident in her expression. "Thank you," she said, her voice tinged with gratitude. "He's been my companion for many years, through thick

and thin." As Stephanie dismounted from Kenco's back, her legs wobbled beneath her, betraying the fatigue that lingered after their long ride.

Without hesitation, I stepped forward, instinctively reaching out to catch her before she could stumble.

Our hands met in mid-air, a fleeting touch that sent a jolt of electricity coursing through me. There was a spark of heat and chemistry between us, undeniable and intoxicating, as our eyes locked in that shared moment of connection.

For a heartbeat, time seemed to stand still. We stood there, suspended in the space between us.

The warmth of Stephanie's hand in mine sent a shiver down my spine, igniting a fire that burned with a fierce intensity. But before I could dwell on the sensation, Stephanie slowly started to pull away, her cheeks flushed with color as she regained her balance. "Thank you," she murmured, her voice barely above a whisper.

Stephanie turned from me, her cheeks flushed and her gaze averted. I felt a surge of longing wash over me—a primal desire that pulsed with a fierce intensity. I knew in that moment that I couldn't let

her go, that I needed to seize the opportunity before it slipped away.

With a sudden surge of boldness, I closed the

distance between us, my hand reaching out to cup Stephanie's chin, gently tilting her face up to meet mine. Our eyes locked once more and I could see uncertainty mingled with desire in her lovely blue eyes. Without a word, I leaned in, capturing her lips in a searing kiss that left no room for hesitation. The taste of her was intoxicating, sweet and spicy—a tantalizing blend of passion and longing that set my senses ablaze.

Stephanie responded eagerly, her hands finding their way to my waist as she melted into me, her body yielding to my touch with a fervent urgency. I could feel the heat of her skin against mine. The electric current that surged between us ignited a fire that burned with a fierce intensity. In that moment, there was no room for doubt or hesitation, only the raw, unbridled passion that consumed us both. I felt a surge of dominance rise within me, a primal need to possess and claim her as my own.

I knew that she felt it too—a shared desire that bound us together in a web of longing and lust. As our kiss deepened, our bodies pressed together in a fervent embrace. I felt a sense of exhilaration wash over me. The freedom and liberation that came from surrendering to the primal instincts that pulsed within us both.

My tongue pushed into her mouth insistently as my hands roamed her body. Every inch of her skin felt electric beneath my touch,

and soft moans of pleasure fell from Stephanie's lips as she surrendered herself to me.

The horses stood by- un-phased by our actions. Out of the corner of my eye I saw them dip their heads to graze the grass beneath their hooves. They would wander a little, but we would get them back later.

The horses were fine. My whole focus went back to her, Stephanie, melting in my arms. I threw her hat to the side. I reached to loosen her belt and pull her plaid shirt from where it was tucked into her jeans. I took hold of the hem of her shirt, lifting it over her head with a sharp tug. I heard buttons pop, but I didn't care. My need for her body was so much greater. Her breasts were full in her black lace bra and I couldn't take my eyes off them. I had thought about them late at night. That was for sure.

"I want you..." I growled into her ear and felt her shudder further. My lips met her earlobe, pulling it with my teeth, sucking it, running my tongue around it. I could taste sweat on her skin. Salty sweat mingling with the sweetness of her desire.

She moaned and the sound of her moans in the open air did something to me.

Fuck, I wanted her and had wanted her badly now since the first time I met her.

I roughly ripped her breasts out of her bra taking a nipple in my mouth, sucking it, running my teeth over it, biting it. Her moans were louder and her breathing quicker.

I had thought right. As I suspected, Captain Stephanie Morley liked to submit sexually. She liked to yield to dominance. She liked it rough.

I pushed her down to on her back the grassy floor and she lay there looking up at me needily still in her jeans and boots and belt with her breasts spilled out of her lace bra. We were right out in the open, most likely alone for miles, but I didn't care if we weren't. I needed to take her now and no sensible thoughts could override that now.

I squinted in the sunlight, removing my hat and throwing it aside. I lowered myself to her, first straddling her hips and running my hands roughly over her torso and breasts enjoying the way her body moved beneath me. Her nipples had hardened to stiff peaks. They were big brown and inviting. I had enjoyed having them in my mouth.

I knew I could feast on her body for hours and I wanted to do that sometime. But not now. I needed to feel her arousal right now. I moved so I could unfasten her belt and her jeans and I lay on top of her along the length of her, my right hand delving inside her jeans, inside her underwear, finding her wetness with my fingers and there was no sweeter feeling than the way my fingers instinctively slid slickly down from her clitoris to between her labia.

Her next moan was loud and guttural and her head tipped back. "Please..." she gasped.

"What do you want, Stephanie?" I asked. There was so much I could give to her and I wanted to give it all. But here, the first time, I figured I would let her choose.

"Pressure on my clit.. make me come with your hand," she murmured.

I had wanted to fuck her properly. And fuck her I would. But not right now. I'd give her what she had asked for.

I moved the weight of my hips above my right hand and pressed firmly down knowing the pressure of the knuckle at the base of my thumb was against her clit. She gasped as she felt it and her breathing got quicker and I knew it was the perfect spot. I held her tightly, the weight of my body pressing into her and ground my hips down against her knowing my hand was grinding against her clit as my fingers cupped down under her vulva. I felt her pubic hair wiry against my hand. I felt her wetness increasing and increasing against my fingers. I ground down in a rhythm with my hips as I dipped my head to kiss her neck claiming her as mine.

I felt her hips move in rhythm with mine, she was reaching for her own pleasure and opening herself up to it and I liked seeing that.

Her breasts were pinned tightly under me.

"You are so wet for me," I growled into her ear. I gave her more pressure through my hand and felt her shudder beneath me. "Come for me, Baby," I said.

With my command in her ear, she exploded into a million colors beneath me and I could feel her pulsing strongly against my hand still tightly cupped around her.

"Ash.. Oh my god.." Her hands gripped desperately onto my plaid shirt as though she was a baby monkey gripping onto me. I felt her orgasm rippling through her whole body. Her breathing was ragged in my ear.

I felt my own desire pulsing hot and hard between my legs and I knew I needed to do something about it.

I adjusted my position slightly until I was straddling her left thigh and I felt the seam of the denim jeans between my legs between my clitoris and her thigh. I ground the weight of myself down against it as I watched her face change with realisation that I was taking my own pleasure from her.

It took merely seconds before I felt the familiar beautiful heat rising from my pussy to my brain. That exquisite moment just before orgasm; I felt it everywhere building and building and then my climax crashed through me suddenly, through every inch of my body while I was still fully clothed.

I cried out into Stephanie's ear and my cry was absorbed by the vast expanse of space around us.

Fuck, this woman. She did things to me, without even doing anything to me. She hadn't even touched me and yet that was the best orgasm I could remember.

There could have, should have been a million thoughts in my head, but instead it was blissfully empty. All I could think and feel was Stephanie beneath me.

She reached her hands to my face and kissed me with absolute tenderness and openness. Her lips were soft and wet and her tongue probed into my mouth slowly and exploitively. I let her kiss me like that because I liked it.

And my own climax confirmed what I had known for a while.

Stephanie Morley was going to flip my world upside down.

9

STEPHANIE

I wandered the ranch, thinking of my passionate encounter with Ashlyn. I couldn't help but revel in the euphoria that enveloped me. It was a blissful haze that clouded my thoughts and filled me with a sense of contentment. With each step, I felt the warmth of the sun on my skin and the gentle breeze caressing my face, as if in silent celebration of the newfound joy that had entered my life. My body hummed with the lingering echoes of our pleasure, a reminder of the intoxicating connection I had shared with Ashlyn.

Our connection had awakened something deep within me, something primal and undeniable that I certainly hadn't felt for many years- if, in fact, ever.

As I walked, lost in the happy haze of my thoughts, I couldn't help but reflect on my past dating life, which had been marked by solitude and introspection. Throughout school and college, I had always been a loner, content to lose myself in my studies and the quiet solitude of my own thoughts. I had never been one to seek out companionship, preferring instead to forge my path and chart my course in life.

It wasn't until I was twenty-one that I had my first dalliance with a woman—an older, married professor, Deborah Vanstone, who taught me many things, both in and out of the classroom. She was striking- beautiful, feminine, dominant; she was harsh and demanding of me. And I had liked it. Most of it. Our affair had been fleeting, a brief moment of passion in an otherwise ordinary existence. As quickly as it had begun, my affair with Deborah had come to an end when I joined the army, leaving behind the confines of academia for the rigors of military life.

And though I had tried to bury the memories of my time with Deborah, they had always lingered in the recesses of my mind.

While in the army, surrounded by the camaraderie of my fellow soldiers and the surge of adrenaline that came with each mission, I had often found myself the object of attention from men. It was a common occurrence. A natural consequence of the male-dominated environment we operated in.

At times, I had entertained the thought of succumbing to the allure of physical intimacy with a man—of satisfying my own needs and desires in the heat of the moment.

But then there had been Jon, a kind and gentle soul who had approached me one evening, his eyes filled with longing and desire, the scent of his sweat and testosterone unmistakably masculine and it did nothing but repulse me. In that fleeting moment, as his lips met mine in a hesitant kiss, I had known with absolute certainty that I could never find satisfaction in the arms of a man.

It wasn't that Jon wasn't attractive or desirable. He was, in his own way. But as our lips touched and his hands roamed over my body, I felt a profound emptiness. A sense of disconnect that left me feeling hollow and unfulfilled.

In that moment, I realized that my body simply wasn't programmed to respond to the touch of a man, no matter how well-intentioned or caring he might be. And though I had tried to bury the memory of that kiss, it was always somehow still there, a silent reminder of the truth that lay at the core of my being.

From that day forward, I had embraced my truth wholeheartedly, accepting myself for who I was and refusing to compromise my own desires for the sake of societal expectations.

Then there was Lieutenant Sophia Clark—a force of nature, a woman unlike any I had ever encountered before.

Strong, fit, and fiercely independent, she exuded an aura of confidence and defiance that captured my attention from the moment our paths crossed in my earlier army days.

From the start, Sophia had dominated my thoughts, her presence looming large in my mind like a beacon in the darkness. I found myself longing for her, yearning to be near her. Wanting to bask in the warmth of her gaze and the strength of her touch.

Every interaction with Sophia had been like a jolt of electricity coursing through my veins, igniting a fire within me that burned with a fierce intensity. I found myself drawn to her, irresistibly caught in the magnetic pull of her presence. Unable to resist her gravitational force.

I would find excuses to spend time with Sophia, seeking out any opportunity to feel the warmth of her smile and the feeling of her fingers inside me. Though I knew that our connection was forbidden, because the army was in the dark ages of Don't Ask, Don't Tell, so our moments were stolen and secret.

Then there was the moment that changed everything.

Although we had never spoken about taking things further, beyond our secret meetings and hidden nights together, I had always just assumed we would. But a few nights before we left the middle east to fly home to the US and we both had two months off coming up, she sat down with me alone in our sleeping quarters.

"Steph, there's something I need to tell you." Her brown eyes were shifty and her full lips that I had enjoyed so much pleasure from kissing were finally spilling out the truth she had been hiding from me. She held my hand in hers and rubbed it with her thumb. "I'm married. His name is Martin. We have been together 4 years. We got married earlier this year. He is army too. He is based up north. I'm going to be spending the next two months with him and then we've asked for our next posting to be together. We will get a house together. Build a home. Have kids."

A home with him? A home? With Martin? Have kids? My head was reeling. *We* had been seeing each other for 3 years. Sure, she always disappeared on me when she had time off, but she told me she was visiting her family. We had been on multiple tours together. *I* wanted her to want a home and kids with me. That was what I wanted with her.

I ripped my hand away from her.

This woman who had loved me so passionately, who had cared for me so deeply when things got scary, didn't really love me. She loved a man.

Or, maybe she didn't *love* him like that. Maybe her desire for women sexually was as genuine as my own. Either way, she didn't love me. Not really. Because when you love someone you don't keep secrets from them. Especially not a secret life. A secret husband. A secret future that certainly didn't involve me.

When the truth finally sank in, a wave of conflicting emotions washed over me—anger, betrayal, and heartbreak, along with a profound sense of disillusionment. I felt like the ground had been

ripped out from under my feet, leaving me adrift in a sea of uncertainty and pain.

I couldn't help but feel betrayed, not just by Sophia, but by myself as well. How had I allowed myself to become entangled in an affair with a married woman? How had I failed to see the signs, to heed the warnings that had been there all along?

"We could, you know, still see each other on occasion- take a holiday together once in a while, be alone together." She picked my hand up again and my blood felt like ice in my veins. She was still happy to use me to satisfy her desires, clearly. But, I would never be her priority and that wasn't enough for me.

Amid the storm of emotions raging inside me, there was also a sense of clarity—a realization that I needed to extricate myself from this situation. To distance myself from Sophia and the turmoil she had brought into my life. With a heavy heart and a resolve born of necessity, I made the difficult decision to end the affair before she left, to sever ties with Sophia and reclaim control over my own life.

"I can't," I whispered. And I could barely look

at her as I said it. It hurt, too much. Everything about this was just too painful. I took my hand back for the second time. And I wished I didn't desperately want her to reach out for me for a third time.

She didn't.

~

The following day felt hollow and I was going through the motions. Sophia went out on patrol as she always did. I stayed back on base and treated the soldiers we had in our medical ward. I felt numb. I felt tears beading in my eyes regularly and I would escape to the bathroom to hide my pain. I felt sick deep down inside. How could I not have known? It turns out most of our friends knew about Martin, but they didn't want to be the ones to tell me.

I wished one of them had told me.

I stood in the bathroom clutching the sink and staring at my gaunt reflection in the mirror and my pager buzzed with the emergency signal. I felt adrenaline begin to course through my veins. I splashed water in my face and headed back out to find out what the emergency was.

"Right, what is the emergency?" I asked as I breezed through trying to ooze professionalism from every pore. I had to pull myself together. My people were going to need me.

Medical staff were busying around. " Captain Morley. I'm prepping the OR," I heard a call from a nurse.

My assistant, Alice Chen had a different look in her eyes. We had worked together a long time and I hadn't seen this look on her face before.

"The morning patrol has been hit. A rescue team is bringing them back now."

I felt my whole body freeze in its tracks. I couldn't focus on anything.

I felt Alice's hand on my arm as around us everything became more frantic and I knew. Of course I knew, deep down inside somewhere before she said the words.

"Captain, its Lieutenent Clark's vehicle. It doesn't sound good."

Of course Alice knew about my relationship with Sophia. Definitely not officially. But, she was intuitive, she knew me well. She would have seen the easy intimacy Sophia and I had that was exclusive to lovers.

"Do you need to sit this one out?" she asked, kindly.

Of course, hospital on an army base didn't work like normal hospital. Most of the time, the patients were someone we knew. I had to pull myself together and get on with it and we both knew that.

I took a deep breath. One. Two. Three. In and out. In and out.

"No, of course not. I'm fine." I heard my own voice as though I was floating above the medical ward.

Alice looked at me full of empathy and we both knew that she knew. We also both knew that I was the most experienced trauma surgeon we had.

"Ok," she said calmly. "I'll help you, Captain. ETA is 3 minutes. Scrub in and prepare for surgery. I'll be right next to you. I'll do my best for you."

My body went through the motions of gowning up and scrubbing in. I stepped into the OR and of course the body on the table was her. Sophia. Who else would it be? A mass of dark hair. Her eyes closed, I remember her beautiful eyelashes. Alice hurriedly went to cover her face with a sheet so I could work on fixing her body.

There was blood. So much blood that I will

never forget. It pooled on the white tiles underneath the table.

Sophia's injuries were catastrophic and she died on my table two hours later. I couldn't save her. I doubt anyone could have.

I staggered out of the OR afterwards covered in her blood and gasping for air. I went outside and screamed into the desert where sand and sky become one.

I knew I had to find a way to hide it. My pain had to be secret, just as our relationship had been.

I hid in my room and cried and cried and cried and I couldn't imagine a way forward from that moment.

~

The memories of Sophia faded over the years. There was a lot about her I would never forget and when I think back, I know the tenderness we shared in the dark nights in the desert was real. Army real anyway. That is the thing about army life. It isn't real life, but it takes you to such intensity of emotion with each other that you build bonds that are so much deeper than real life.

I went to war with Sophia Clark by my side. I

tended the injured and had friends die in front of me. Sophia was the one holding me at night when I cried in the dark.

That was real.

Sophia was the one next to me when we went on missions and I was afraid. I hid it well. Of course I did. We all did. Sophia would squeeze my thigh as we sat together in the back of a truck, not knowing what we would find when we arrived where we were going, so I would know I wasn't alone. We had each other's back.

That was real.

When we kissed. When we had sex. Her lust. Her desire for me.

It was real. I know it was.

So, I have chosen to focus on the good. Remember fondly what was, instead of what might have been.

Sophia Clark with her dark hair, dark eyes, full sensual lips, body that I couldn't rip my eyes away from- she sits in a box somewhere in my mind and I don't delve into it often.

~

Since having my home on the ranch, the comforting routines of caring for the animals and tending to the land are a solace for me. For a time, the ranch became my sanctuary, a place of refuge where I could find peace amid the chaos of my past. I had convinced myself that I didn't need a woman in my life. That I could find fulfillment and contentment within the quiet solitude of the ranch.

And for a while, it had worked. I had thrown myself into my work, losing myself in the daily tasks and responsibilities that came with running the ranch. The memories of my past life in the army faded into the background and I found solace in the tranquility of the ranch, taking injured or traumatised animals and nursing them back to health. The brokenness of the animals mirrored my own inner struggles. In their presence, I found a sense of purpose and fulfillment. I was able to lose myself in the simple rhythms of caring for their needs and tending to the land.

I had learned to satisfy my own sexual desires with my right hand in my own bed. It was enough for me. For all those years, it was enough.

But now Ashlyn had entered my life like a wildfire, setting ablaze the carefully constructed walls I had erected around my heart. From the moment she arrived, Ashlyn stirred something within me—a passion and desire that I had long thought extinguished. Her presence was like a bolt of lightning, electrifying the air with an intensity that left me breathless and yearning for more.

Sure, in some ways she reminded me of Sophia. Although aside from their hair, they didn't look similar. But they shared an undefinable charisma and a sensuality that are rarely found.

With each passing encounter, Ashlyn stoked the fire within me—a primal, insatiable hunger that threatened to consume me whole. Her touch was like a drug, intoxicating and addictive, leaving me craving more with every fleeting caress. And though I tried to resist the pull of attraction that simmered between us, I found myself powerless to deny the magnetic force that repeatedly drew me to her.

As I watched Ashlyn tend to Phantom, a nervous energy pulsed through me. My desire to spend more time with her grew stronger with each passing moment. Though I had never been one to shy away from taking the lead, the prospect of asking Ashlyn out on a date filled me with trepidation.

But, I knew I didn't want another secret relationship, as exciting as the passion between us was. I wanted something real if I was going to have something. Real world real.

Summoning every ounce of courage I could muster, I approached Ashlyn tentatively, my heart pounding in my chest as I struggled to find the right words. "Um, Ashlyn?" I began, my voice wavering slightly with uncertainty. "I was wondering if, uh, you might like to, um, go out with me sometime? Like, a date." The words hung in the air between us, heavy with anticipation as I waited for Ashlyn's response. Would she say yes? Or would she politely decline, leaving me to wallow in embarrassment and disappointment?

To my relief, Ashlyn's face broke into a warm smile, her green eyes sparkling like emeralds with genuine interest. "I would love to," she replied, her voice soft and inviting. A rush of relief flooded through me, accompanied by a surge of excitement at the prospect of spending time alone with Ashlyn. Anticipation built within me—as well as a flicker of hope that maybe, just maybe, this could be the beginning of something special between us.

10

ASHLYN

I settled into one of the small outbuildings on the ranch, but couldn't fix the restlessness stirring within me. The house's sparse furnishings and lack of personal belongings left it feeling empty and devoid of warmth. A stark reminder of just how far removed I was from the comforts of Brooks Creek life.

With a sigh, I glanced around the room, taking in the bare walls and the simple decor with a sense of unease. I longed for the familiar sights and sounds of the bustling town—the crowded streets and luxury brands. But here on the ranch, there were no big stores or trendy boutiques to satisfy my craving for retail therapy. The nearest town was miles away, its small shops and quaint storefronts offering little in the way of the designer labels and luxury brands that I had grown accustomed to.

Frustration gnawed at me as I contemplated my limited options. Honestly, the prospect of spending my days surrounded by nothing but nature and solitude felt suffocating. I yearned for the excitement of a shopping spree, the thrill of discovering new treasures and indulging in the latest fashion trends.

But resignation washed over me as I gazed out at the sprawling expanse of the ranch. This was my new reality and I would have to learn to adapt to it, whether I liked it or not.

Then, there was Stephanie. I couldn't stop thinking about our encounter and the way she felt when she orgasmed beneath me. She was like a drug to me. I knew I wanted more and more.

My thoughts inevitably turned to Stephanie and the upcoming date we had planned. Despite my initial reservations about mixing business with pleasure, there was an undeniable pull drawing me toward her. I couldn't help but marvel at how easily I had agreed to the date, her shy invitation belying a quiet confidence that intrigued me. There was something about Stephanie—something genuine and sincere—that spoke to me on a deeper level. I felt a spark of curiosity and interest that I hadn't experienced in a long time.

As I contemplated the prospect of spending time with her, excitement bubbled up within me, tempered only by the nagging doubt that lingered at the back of my mind. I knew that getting involved with my new boss could complicate things, especially considering the delicate balance of relationships and dynamics at play.

But even as I wrestled with my doubts, I couldn't shake the feeling that this was something worth pursuing. There was a connection between us. A shared understanding and mutual respect. It felt rare and precious. A hidden treasure in the midst of a vast wilderness.

I rummaged through my modest wardrobe, searching for something suitable to wear on my date with Stephanie. I was excited. The warm rays of the sun filtered through the window, casting a golden glow over the room and filling me with a renewed sense of joy.

After much deliberation, I started with matching panties and bra in a dark red silk. I've always been a fan of underwear. I can remember sweetly in my mind the black lace bra as I tore Stephanie's breasts from it. The thought of

Stephanie's reaction to seeing me in this silk underwear excited me. I knew she liked my body. I had seen the hunger in her eyes as her gaze ran approvingly up and down scanning my muscles, the curves of my breasts and ass, the length of my legs.

For the rest of my outfit, I opted for comfort and casual elegance. A pair of my favorite denim shorts that I knew made my ass look great. I matched it with a soft, cotton tank top that offered just the right amount of coverage. Oh, and some exceptional boots and my favorite hat, of course. Because the evening air could get chilly, I grabbed a button-up sweater that I could throw over my shoulders, its soft fabric providing a comforting layer of warmth against the chill.

With a satisfied nod, I surveyed myself in the mirror, pleased with my choice of attire. The outfit was simple yet stylish. A reflection of my laid-back personality and the casual nature of our date. I made my way out the door, eager to see where the evening would take us and what adventures awaited on the edge of the ranch.

As I stepped out of the little ranch house I now called home, my heart fluttered with anticipation about the evening ahead. The warm breeze tousled my hair as I made my way across the sprawling expanse of the ranch, the familiar sights and sounds of nature soothing my nerves and filling me with a sense of calm.

When I passed Melody, a sense of curiosity tugged at me, prompting me to offer her a friendly wave. To my surprise, she returned the gesture with a knowing smile, eyes twinkling with a hint of mischief that piqued my interest. For someone so young, Melody seemed to possess a keen intuition and a deep understanding of the dynamics between the people on the ranch. There was wisdom in her gaze, plus a silent acknowledgment of unspoken bond that connected us all.

I couldn't help but wonder what secrets Melody held. What insights she possessed that made her seem so attuned to the world around her. But the thought faded into the background as I walked, overshadowed by my excitement about my impending rendezvous with Stephanie. I quickened my pace, eager to see what the evening had in store. Ready to embrace whatever adventures awaited me.

11

STEPHANIE

As I waited for Ashlyn to arrive for our date, my mind buzzed with a mixture of excitement and nervous anticipation. Her simple act of agreeing to a date, and the look in her eyes when she did it, had sent my thoughts into a whirlwind. I felt both excited and nervous about what the evening might bring.

I kept replaying the moment she said "yes" over and over again in my mind, each time feeling a flutter of excitement in the pit of my stomach. There was something about her response that felt different, something that set Ashlyn apart from anyone else I had encountered. I generally prided myself on my organization and meticulous planning, but the prospect of a date with Ashlyn had thrown me off balance in the most unexpected way. Normally, I'd have mapped out every detail, from the venue to the activities—but with her, all my carefully laid plans seemed irrelevant.

I found myself Googling, reading blogs, and attempting to envision a perfect first date, but nothing seemed to capture what I truly desired, which was an unfiltered, uninterrupted moment of connection with Ashlyn. It was as if the simplicity of just being in her presence was all I needed to feel complete.

At the same time, my doubts had begun to creep in again. What if she didn't feel the same way? What if my attempts at simplicity fell short of her expectations? The fear of rejection loomed large in my mind, threatening to overshadow the budding excitement within me. But as I smoothed out the edges of a worn chequered blanket and felt the soft blades of spring grass beneath my fingertips, I realized that my heart had already made its decision. *What could go wrong*, I wondered, *when the possibility of being with Ashlyn felt so right?*

Questions danced in my mind as I waited for Ashlyn's arrival. I wondered how she would smile when she found me there. How she would react to my simple gesture of feeding her a strawberry. I wondered about the taste of melted ice cream on her fingers. But above all, I wondered about the possibility of Ashlyn kissing me again—of experiencing the electric connection that seemed to crackle in the air whenever our eyes met.

When I first caught sight of her, a rush of admiration washed over me. Ashlyn looked stunning, her outfit exuding an effortless charm and beauty that drew my gaze like a magnet. I couldn't help but appreciate the way the sunlight played off her features, casting a soft glow that highlighted her natural allure.

Her choice of attire, a combination of shorts, a tank top, and a light button-down sweater, seemed perfectly suited for the warm Texan weather, and it allowed her to move with ease and grace. Every detail, from the way Ashlyn's hair fell in loose waves to the subtle curve of her smile, only served to enhance her presence.

She drew nearer, and I couldn't help but stand to greet her, my heart fluttering with anticipation at the prospect of spending time with this beautiful woman. My own outfit, a light skirt and a simple button-down shirt, paled in comparison to

Ashlyn's effortless elegance, but I felt a sense of comfort in its simplicity.

With a smile on my lips, I welcomed Ashlyn with open arms, feeling a surge of warmth and excitement at the thought of our upcoming date. As we settled onto the picnic blanket, a comfortable silence enveloped us, interrupted only by the gentle rustle of leaves and the distant chirping of birds. It felt strangely comforting to be in each other's presence. As if we had known each other for years, rather than for mere moments.

"So, Stephanie," Ashlyn began, her voice soft and inviting, "what's your favorite color?"

I couldn't help but smile at her simple question, and at the easy way she sought to connect with me. "I'd have to say blue," I replied, my gaze drifting to the sky above us, where wispy clouds painted delicate patterns against an azure expanse. "There's just something so calming about it, don't you think? Like the sky. The ocean."

"Like your eyes," Ashlyn responded simply as she looked into them. I knew I could lose myself in Ashlyn's eyes.

Ashlyn nodded thoughtfully as she looked up. "I can see that," she agreed, her voice filled with genuine interest. "For me, it's definitely green. I love the way it represents growth and renewal, like endless possibilities stretching out before me."

Ashlyn's words resonated with me, stirring something deep within my soul. "That's beautiful," I murmured, feeling a kind of kinship as we shared our thoughts and dreams beneath the open sky. The conversation flowed effortlessly between us, so we delved deeper into each other's lives, sharing stories and secrets with an openness that felt both exhilarating and liberating. We talked about our most cherished memories, our wildest dreams, and the places we longed to explore.

"I've always wanted to travel to Italy," I confessed, my eyes alight with excitement at the thought of exploring its ancient ruins and sampling its delectable cuisine. "There's just something so enchanting about the culture and history there."

Ashlyn's face lit up with a smile, her eyes sparkling with curiosity. "Italy sounds amazing," she agreed, her voice tinged with excitement. "I've always been drawn to Japan myself. The vibrant culture, the breathtaking landscapes—it's like stepping into another world."

We laughed and joked together, our laughter

mingling with the gentle breeze as we basked in the warmth of each other's company. With each passing moment, I felt myself growing closer to Ashlyn, feeling our connection deepen with every shared revelation and touch. The sun began to dip below the horizon, casting a golden glow over the landscape, and I found myself lost in the moment, completely at ease in Ashlyn's presence.

With a playful smile, I reached into the picnic basket and began to unpack our makeshift feast, laying out the strawberries, ice cream, and drinks with care. The tantalizing aroma of freshly picked fruit filled the air, mingling with the sweet scent of vanilla from the melting ice cream. I glanced up and caught Ashlyn's eye. A smile passed between us, sparking a warmth in my chest that I couldn't quite explain. It felt exhilarating to be sharing this moment with her, to be basking in the glow of her presence as we indulged in our simple feast.

"So, tell me, Ashlyn," I began, my voice soft with curiosity, "have you always had a sweet tooth, or is it just for special occasions like this?"

Ashlyn chuckled, her laughter like music to my ears as she reached for a strawberry, her fingers brushing against mine in the process. "I'll admit; I've always had a weakness for sweets," she confessed, her eyes twinkling with mischief. "But there's something about sharing them with someone special that makes them taste even better."

Her words sent a shiver down my spine, a rush of warmth flooding my cheeks as I met her gaze. In that moment, it felt as though the world had faded away, leaving only the two of us, lost in a sea of shared laughter and stolen glances. As we continued to chat and flirt, our conversation flowing effortlessly, I found myself drawn to Ashlyn in a way I had never experienced before. With each passing moment, our closeness grew. Our laughter mingled with the gentle breeze as we leaned closer to each other, our words and touches becoming increasingly intimate.

Lost in the magic of the moment, I reached for a spoonful of ice cream, offering it to Ashlyn with a playful grin. "Care to share?" I asked, my heart fluttering with anticipation as I awaited her response.

She met my gaze with a smile, her eyes sparkling with warmth and affection. Her dark hair was loose around her shoulders and I just wanted to run my fingers through it. "I'd love to," she replied, her voice soft and full of promise. Our faces got closer until finally our spoons met in the middle, and we were sharing the sweet taste of ice cream and the warmth of our connection. The anticipation was killing me. The tension grew as the space between us narrowed. Finally, there was barely a breath of air separating our lips.

I couldn't resist the pull any longer. With a soft sigh, I leaned in, closing the gap as our lips met in a tender, electrifying kiss. It was as though time stood still, the world around us fading into oblivion as we lost ourselves in the heat of the moment. The taste of ice cream lingered on our lips, mingling with a heady rush of desire.

Before I knew it, she was pushing me back until my back was on the blanket and she was on top of me again. I heard myself gasp in the pleasure of it. Feeling the weight of her body on top of my own was the most exquisite pleasure. I felt taken back immediately to the orgasm she had given me easily with her hand only days before.

Her right thigh moved between my own to part my legs and press tightly into me. I felt the invasion of it and I liked it. Ashlyn's face hovered above my own. Her hair falling down onto me. In the golden light of the setting sun her beauty was incomparable.

"Tonight, I'm going to take my time with you,"

she said, her green eyes glittering with desire. "I was impatient, the other day. But now, I want to worship your body with my mouth. I want to taste you." I felt a deep buzz running through my body in delicious anticipation. "Then I want to fuck you until you come and come and come again." I thought I might come there and then, just feeling her body pressing into mine and hearing her words.

But, I didn't.

I wanted her to take me like that so very badly. But, I was also so scared. It had been years since I had had sex. She turned me on so much and I was deep in desire, but what if my body didn't respond as I wanted it to?

"I.. I want to so badly." I said. "But, I have to be honest. It has been a very long time since I had sex. And I just don't know how I will be. But, I want to so very much."

She held my face in her hands and looked sincerely into my eyes. "Then I'll be as gentle as you need me to be. I'll go so slowly and at any time, if there is anything that you don't like or don't feel comfortable with, you just stop me. Ok?"

I nodded. "Ok," I breathed. "I trust you,

Ashlyn," I said and she held me close and kissed me tenderly.

She moved down my body slowly and carefully removing my clothes until I lay naked beneath her. I thought I might feel more shy when she stripped my bra and panties from me, but I didn't. With her, it felt like the most natural thing in the world.

She kissed me as she went. She ran her tongue over me. I felt like the most beautiful woman in the world under her touch. Her tongue met my pussy and licked with long slow licks, teasing and exciting me with every stroke. I had no doubt she knew exactly what she was doing. I looked up a the vast sky above and relaxed and opened my legs to her. I knew I would let her take me in every way.

"I want to see you, too," I said, sitting up and pulling at her shirt. Last time Ashlyn had remained fully dressed and I had wished desperately that I had seen her body, wished I had had opportunity to touch her.

She smiled lazily and stripped slowly out of the denim shorts and loose shirt. Her body was exposed to me, beautiful in dark red silk underwear as she straddled my hips and sat astride me as though I was a wild horse she was taming.

"More," I murmured, mesmerized.

Ashlyn grinned. Her smile was dazzling. She was more attractive than anyone I could have imagined. She unfastened her bra and my eyes couldn't be dragged away from her breasts as they fell free. Small, firm, perfect breasts with small pink nipples that my mouth instinctively reached for.

The flat of her palm touched my chest as she pushed me back down.

"Not yet, sweetheart," she said and her voice was husky and sexier than ever. She stood up so that she could peel her way out of the dark red silk panties and I happily watched her. Her lithe athletic body stood above me silhouetted against the sun. I could see the dark of her pubic hair between her legs and I longed to bury my face there.

But, I knew she wanted to take me first and as much as I had worried, I knew I would be fine with it. She knelt between my legs and her fingers teased at my vulva, running through my wetness, threatening persistently to penetrate me.

"Are you ready, my darling," she whispered and I felt desperate to feel her inside me. I nodded and I felt her fingers pushing inside me. Deeply. Firmly. Perfectly.

"Are you ok?" she asked.

"Yes," I answered. "You feel so good."

Her fingers began to move in response, curling up, finding my G spot. Beginning to take a rhythm and move in and out as they began to fuck me.

I found my body responding for me with deep moans and quickened breathing. My legs parted further for her.

"More..." I gasped and she smiled again.

"Needy, sweet girl," she growled. She added another finger and fucked me harder than before and I liked every second of it.

I felt my body jolting as she fucked me. I wanted more. I wanted harder. I wanted to lose myself forever in this feeling of being fucked.

"Harder..." I murmured.

"Oh baby, I thought you would never ask," she responded and I felt suddenly more stretched by her, I felt like she was ramming herself into my body to take me completely and I wanted to go all the way there with her.

I felt my orgasm building deep inside me.

"I'm so close," I gasped.

There had been plenty of times with past lovers that my orgasm had been hard to reach-most likely down to my overthinking. That certainly wasn't the case with Ashlyn- far from it.

"Come for me, Baby, come for my fingers fucking you," she purred and her thumb pressed against my clitoris. The sound of her filthy words tipped me over the edge and my body exploded in climax in response. Pleasure radiated through every part of me.

I couldn't imagine anything ever being this good. Her fingers slid slowly out of me and she lay on top of me and kissed me tenderly.

"You are so beautiful," she said and I felt warmth flooding my body.

I felt her wetness against my thigh.

I moved my hand, my fingers seeking her out to give her pleasure in return.

"Your mouth, baby," she murmured. "Can I come in your mouth?"

"Yes," my response was eager, perhaps too quick and she raised an eyebrow. But, she didn't hesitate. She moved to straddle my face and I buried my face in her, my tongue working eagerly to please her, tasting the sweet muskiness of her, licking every part of her, losing myself in her wetness until she cried out and came hard on my tongue gripping a handful of my hair as she did.

"Fuck, Steph," she said as she relaxed her grip and moved off my face finally.

Mostly I don't let people call me Steph. But she did and I liked it.

It seemed as though there had never been a past and would be no future. Only the present mattered—the intoxicating thrill of being lost in each other's embrace.

12

ASHLYN

The morning sun filtered through the curtains, casting a warm glow across the room as I lay there, lost in thought. The events of last night played over in my mind like a reel of film, each moment etched into my memory with crystal clarity. It had been the best date I had ever been on, hands down.

As I lay there, I couldn't help but feel a sense of contentment wash over me. Being with Stephanie felt . . . right, in a way that I hadn't experienced before. There was a comfort in her presence, a familiarity that made me feel at ease in a way that I hadn't felt in a long time.

But along with that comfort came a sense of unease, a nagging voice in the back of my mind warning me of the dangers that lay ahead. I knew that getting involved with Stephanie could complicate things, not just for me but for her as well. We came from different worlds, but I couldn't shake the feeling that our paths were destined to diverge. And despite the risks, I found myself drawn to her in a way that I couldn't ignore. There was something about Stephanie that called to me, something I couldn't resist. It wasn't just her beauty or her intelligence, though both were undeniable. It was something deeper, something intangible that spoke to my soul on a level that I couldn't fully comprehend.

As much as I wanted to explore those feelings, to see where they might lead, I needed to proceed with caution. I couldn't afford to let my emotions run wild, not when there was so much at stake. And so, as I lay there in the quiet of the morning, I vowed to tread carefully. To guard my heart against the inevitable storm that lay ahead.

My thoughts drifted from Stephanie to Phantom, and I couldn't help but feel a surge of pride at the progress we had made together. In the short time since I had taken on the role of his trainer, he had grown by leaps and bounds, responding to my guidance and commands with a level of trust and obedience that I hadn't anticipated. But along with that progress came a new set of challenges, because Phantom's newfound confidence and skill demanded more from me as his trainer. No longer content with simple exercises and routines, I knew the next step was preparing him for competitions.

While part of me relished the thought of taking the horse to races, showcasing his talent to the world, another part of me hesitated, aware of the potential dangers. The world of horse racing was fraught with risks, both physical and emotional, and I couldn't shake the feeling that I was leading Phantom into uncharted territory. That plus the threat that lingered over me from the past.

But I also remembered that when I had looked into his eyes, I had seen the fire of determination burning bright. A hunger for success that mirrored my own. In that moment, I knew that I couldn't hold him back. I had to trust in his abilities, and in my own as his trainer. I continued to think about the path ahead for Phantom and me.

However, nagging thought soon crept in, casting a shadow over my newfound optimism. The looming decision about the severance package I had received from my former employer. It was a tempting offer that promised financial security in exchange for my silence. The terms of the agreement were clear: I was to accept a substantial sum of money and agree never to speak of my time at Brooks Creek, nor to seek employment within the state of Kentucky. This would eliminate any trace of my past and would allow me to start anew.

But as I considered the implications of such an arrangement, unease settled in the pit of my stomach. What if I was found out anyway? What if someone were to uncover the truth of my past, unearthing the secrets I had buried deep within? The consequences could be catastrophic, not only for me, but for Phantom and Stephanie as well. If my past with Monica were to come to light, it could jeopardize everything we had worked so hard to build together, casting a shadow of doubt and suspicion over our fledgling relationship.

If I accepted the agreement, I could start over again with a clean slate. Still, I hesitated.

Something within me rebelled against the idea of sacrificing my freedom for the sake of financial gain and allowing myself to be bound by the chains of secrecy and deceit.

The problem was that if Phantom ever qualified for the biggest race of all- the Kentucky Derby, which I knew was a possibility, I wouldn't be able to take him there because I would have signed papers to keep me out of the state. And Phantom was the kind of horse who could go far. Phantom was going to be a champion and he would need me there beside him.

That was my gut feeling about him, anyway. You could never be too sure. Phantom could hate the spotlight, or he could be distracted by the crowds. Or maybe it would all be too much for him.

Eventually, I made the decision to accept the terms of the agreement and to embrace the risk and uncertainty that lay ahead. For better or for worse, it was my ticket to redemption, my chance to prove myself. And I needed to talk to Stephanie.

∽

As I watched her approach, warmth washed over me, banishing the doubts and worries that had plagued my mind. In that moment, all thoughts of Phantom and the agreement faded into the background, replaced by the simple joy of being in Stephanie's presence.

Her smile was like sunshine on a cloudy day,

bright and infectious, lighting up the space between us with its radiant warmth. As she drew nearer, I couldn't help but marvel at the grace and poise with

which she moved, a testament to the strength and resilience that lay within her.

I greeted Stephanie with a smile of my own, my heart swelling with affection as I offered her the breakfast I had gone to such lengths to acquire. It had involved an hour round-trip into town, to the bakery. A small gesture, but one that felt significant in its simplicity. A tangible expression of my desire to make her happy.

It was easy to feel the electricity between us. We talked and laughed, sharing stories and dreams with a newfound ease and intimacy. This felt both exhilarating and terrifying. But there was also an undercurrent of longing that pulsed beneath the surface, a silent yearning that begged to be acknowledged. I found myself drawn to Stephanie in ways I couldn't fully comprehend, my heart racing with a mixture of excitement and apprehension in her presence.

I felt alive in a way I hadn't in years, my senses heightened and emotions laid bare. She had a way of seeing straight through me, of stripping away the layers of pretense and self-doubt, to reveal the true essence of who I was. We sat there together, basking in the glow of each other's company, and I knew with a certainty that defied logic that Stephanie was something special. Sitting across from her, I couldn't help but feel a rush of excitement as she prepared to share her past with me. Her eyes held a hint of vulnerability, yet I sensed a quiet determination within her that drew me in.

"So, you want to know about my time in the army?" Stephanie began, her voice soft, but filled with a sense of purpose.

I nodded eagerly, leaning in closer to catch every word she spoke. "Absolutely. I'm all ears."

Stephanie's smile was warm as she began to recount her journey. "Well, it feels like a lifetime ago now, but it all started right after college. I wanted to make a difference, you know?"

Listening intently, I nodded, captivated by her story. "I can definitely understand that," I said. "What made you decide to become an army doctor?"

Stephanie's gaze drifted as she spoke. "It was a combination of things, really. I wanted to serve my country and being a doctor seemed like the best way to do that. Plus, I've always had a passion for medicine."

As Stephanie shared her experiences, I found myself drawn deeper into her world. I realized I was hanging on to her every word. "That makes sense," I said encouragingly. "It must have been quite the journey."

Stephanie's smile softened, her eyes reflecting a mix of emotions. "It was. There were moments of both triumph and hardship, but overall, my path shaped me into the person I am today."

Admiring Stephanie's strength, I reached out, lightly touching her hand. "I am impressed by your strength, Stephanie. It takes a special kind of person to serve in the army."

A blush spread across Stephanie's cheeks at the compliment, gratitude evident in her eyes.

"Thank you, Ashlyn. That means a lot, coming from you."

Returning her smile, I felt a warmth spread through me, the connection between us growing stronger with each passing moment. "Of course. I genuinely mean it. You're incredibly brave and resilient."

Stephanie's joy was palpable as she met my gaze. "That's really sweet of you to say. It hasn't always been easy, but I wouldn't change a thing." We shared a moment of comfortable silence, and I couldn't help but feel grateful for the opportunity to get to know Stephanie on a deeper level.

"So, what was your proudest experience during your time in the army?" I asked, unable to contain my curiosity.

Stephanie's eyes lit up as she recalled her past adventures. "Oh, there are so many to choose from. But I those that stick in my mind are the lives I saved under difficult circumstances. Performing surgery in the field. Being the difference between life and death."

I couldn't imagine it. A war zone. Injured soldiers. Stephanie rushing in. "Wow, that sounds intense. I can't even imagine. But, you have that about you. That calmness under pressure. I can imagine you were pretty good at saving lives."

Stephanie's warm smile filled the room but she was holding something back, I could see it in her eyes. "It was definitely a unique experience. But it also taught me a lot about myself and what I'm capable of."

"Why did you leave the army," I asked and a shadow crossed her face, and she seemed to retreat into herself. Her eyes clouded over with a hint of sadness. "I . . . I'm not ready to talk about that yet," Stephanie replied, her voice barely above a whisper.

I could sense the walls she had erected around her past, a barrier she wasn't yet ready to dismantle. Respectful of her boundaries, I nodded understandingly. "That's okay, Stephanie. You don't have to tell me if you're not comfortable."

A mixture of relief and gratitude flickered across Stephanie's features as she met my gaze. "Thank you, Ashlyn. It's just . . . it's still a bit raw, you know?"

I reached out, gently squeezing her hand in a silent gesture of support. "I understand. Take all the time you need. I'm here whenever you're ready to talk."

Stephanie's smile returned, albeit a bit subdued. "Thank you for being so understanding."

There was silence for just a moment.

"How about relationships," I asked, desperate to change the subject for her.

She snapped back to normal and laughed, "Well, I've never done very well on that front. There was a woman once, Deborah, my professor at university. We were very different. She was a lot older. It phased out when I joined the army. And, to be honest, it was for the best. She was a demanding bitch. And as much as that turned me on, it wasn't really healthy."

I tried to imagine her with an older professor and I could kind of see it.

"And, then there were women in the army. Mostly insignificant. You know, it was Don't Ask, Don't tell. So, really I never pursued anything serious until Sophia."

"Sophia?" I questioned.

She sighed, deeply.

"Sophia was the one I thought I would marry and live happily ever after with. I loved her desperately. We were so close. We shared such a bond and we went through some terrible things together during our army careers. Only, it turned out Sophia had a husband and had been lying to me all along. The future I had envisioned for us was all a lie- she already had that planned out with her husband. And I was just..." she gazed off into the distance, she was a million miles away. "I was just something. I don't know. A distraction on the long lonely nights in the desert perhaps. A friend when she needed one..." Stephanie looked so desperately sad.

I felt a gnawing sensation at the pit of my

stomach knowing I was hiding things from her too. Maybe not a husband, but nevertheless a sordid past.

"Anyway, what about your past relationships?" she turned back to me.

Here was where I should have come clean. But, I didn't.

"Oh, you know. Nothing too significant. I guess the horses were always my priority."

Spineless idiot.

"Did you always want to become a horse trainer?" she asked.

"You know, I didn't always plan on becoming a horse trainer," I began, my voice tinged with a hint of nostalgia. "It all started when I was a kid. My older brothers used to tease me, saying that girls couldn't control a horse like they could. We grew up surrounded by horses, you see."

Stephanie's eyes widened with curiosity, a small smile playing at the corners of her lips. "Really? And what did you do?"

I chuckled, the memories flooding back. "I was stubborn, I guess. I didn't like being told that I couldn't do something, just because I was a girl. So I begged my parents to let me learn."

Stephanie's smile grew wider, a genuine

warmth emanating from her. "And did you prove your brothers wrong?"

I nodded, pride swelling within me. "Oh, absolutely. Not only did I prove them wrong, but I also fell in love with riding. There's something about being on horseback, feeling the wind in your

hair and the power beneath you. It's like nothing else in the world."

Stephanie listened intently, her gaze never leaving mine. "I feel the same," she remarked, her voice soft with admiration.

"And now, here I am, following my passion and doing what I love every day." As we continued to talk, I felt a sense of connection growing between us, strengthened by our shared experiences and mutual understanding. In that moment, I knew that opening up to Stephanie had been the right choice, a good way to deepen our bond.

13

STEPHANIE

Reflecting on the whirlwind of emotions that had consumed me over the past few days, I couldn't quite believe how quickly things had changed between Ashlyn and me. From our first meeting at the fair to the sexual encounters, to our heartfelt conversations at the ranch, each moment had left an indelible mark on me.

The date had been nothing short of magical, a perfect blend of simplicity and intimacy that had allowed us to connect on a deeper level. As we sat together on the picnic blanket, exchanging stories and sharing laughs, I'd felt a warmth radiating from Ashlyn that had enveloped me in a cocoon of comfort and affection.

And then there had been the sex. Oh, the sex. Her hands were magical in what they could do and had done to me. I just wanted her more and more of it.

But within the blissful haze of newfound love, there lingered a shadow of uncertainty, a nagging doubt that threatened to dampen the joyous spirit of our budding romance. It was the question of

my past, of the secrets I carried within me from my time in the army. The hidden knowledge weighed heavily on my mind, leaving me feeling vulnerable and exposed.

Ashlyn had probed gently about my reasons for leaving the army, but I found myself struggling to find the words to explain, to articulate the pain and trauma that had driven me to seek the solace of the ranch. My memories were still raw, even years later, the wounds still tender, and the thought of reliving those painful moments filled me with a sense of dread.

"I'm not ready to talk about it yet," I finally admitted, my voice barely above a whisper as I met Ashlyn's gaze with a mixture of sadness and apprehension.

In that moment, I saw the genuine concern and

understanding reflected back at me in Ashlyn's eyes. And as she shared fragments of her own past with me, I couldn't help but feel grateful for her willingness to open up and confide in me. Her stories of defying gender stereotypes and finding solace in the company of horses resonated deeply with me. I found myself hanging on her every word, captivated by the strength and resilience she exuded.

But within the tales of her childhood and her journey to becoming the accomplished equestrian Ashlyn was today, there was a shadow of uncertainty due to the looming question of Phantom. This was a topic that had been on my mind ever since Ashlyn had arrived at the ranch. It had become like a silent presence that hovered in the background, waiting to be acknowledged.

Whenever the conversation turned to Phantom, I couldn't help but feel a surge of curiosity mingled with apprehension. I had seen the potential within the spirited horse and felt the raw power and energy that pulsed through his veins. However, I also knew the risks involved in pushing him too far, too fast.

"Tell me about Phantom," I prompted gently,

my voice tinged with a mixture of anticipation and concern. "What do you see for him? What are your plans?" A renowned horse trainer, she should be able to give me a better picture now.

"We have to get him racing. He is fast- I cross checked the times we took for him on the track. It is in his blood, of course. He looks so much like his father, Obsidian Storm and he runs like him too. And then, well, let's see what he qualifies for. See how he likes it."

But beneath her confident exterior, I sensed a flicker of doubt, a hint of vulnerability that belied her stoic facade. It was clear that Phantom held a special place in Ashlyn's heart and the thought of that made me happy.

As Ashlyn spoke, I found myself drawn to the passion and determination that shone in her eyes. Her unwavering belief in Phantom's abilities mirrored my own hopes and dreams for the future. She patiently addressed each of my questions, and I couldn't help but feel a sense of gratitude for her guidance and expertise. Ashlyn's calm demeanor and thoughtful responses reassured me,

easing any lingering concerns I had about Phantom's future.

"What if Phantom isn't a derby horse?" I asked, my voice tinged with uncertainty.

Ashlyn's response was reassuring. "Every horse is unique, Stephanie," she replied, her tone confident yet compassionate. "While I have every confidence in Phantom's abilities, it's

important to remember that not every racehorse will make the Kentucky Derby- it is the biggest race in the states. If he doesn't excel in competitive racing, we'll find another path for him —one that plays to his strengths and allows him to thrive." Her words resonated with me, offering a sense of comfort and perspective. I nodded, silently

acknowledging her wisdom.

"Look how far we have come, already. Most of the time he is calm now, easier to manage, rideable- mostly. Phantom will have a future, but whether it is amongst the stars is yet to be determined."

Next, I asked about the financial aspect of training and competing a horse at the Derby level.

"How much would it cost?" I asked, my gaze steady as I awaited Ashlyn's response.

She took a moment to gather her thoughts before replying. "Training and competing a horse to that level can be a significant investment," she explained, her voice calm, yet confident. "There are costs associated with everything—as soon as we start going to the track and race meets. And you can't forget entry fees and travel expenses. But with the right strategy and support, I believe we can manage the financial aspect effectively and ensure that Phantom has everything he needs to succeed. At least with me you are getting a bargain," she laughed.

Ashlyn's assurance was settling. I felt a renewed sense of confidence in our ability to navigate the financial challenges ahead. As we continued to speak about this, she outlined the steps we would take to begin Phantom's training journey. Ashlyn's enthusiasm was contagious, and I found myself becoming increasingly excited about the possibilities that lay ahead.

However, I had another concern. "Could this type of training set him back?" I asked, my voice laced with apprehension. Ashlyn's response was thoughtful and empathetic. "There's always the possibility of setbacks in any endeavor, Stephanie," she replied gently. "But with careful planning and attentive care, we can minimize the risks and ensure that Phantom's progress remains steady and consistent. It's all about finding the right balance and listening to what Phantom needs along the way."

Her words resonated with me, offering a sense of reassurance and confidence in our ability to overcome any obstacles that might arise. However, I did notice that Ashlyn's positive words contradicted her somewhat closed body language. Perhaps something was wrong. "What about you?" I asked softly, looking her right in the eyes as I did.

Ashlyn's expression softened, her gaze meeting mine with a mixture of surprise and vulnerability.

"What about me?" she echoed, her voice tinged with curiosity.

I hesitated for a moment, the weight of my question hanging in the air between us. "You've shared so much with me about Phantom and your plans for him," I began, my tone gentle, yet probing. "But what about your own dreams and aspirations? What do you hope to achieve through all of this?"

There was a flicker of hesitation in Ashlyn's eyes, a brief moment of uncertainty before she composed herself. "I suppose . . . I hope to see Phantom reach his full potential," she replied, her words carefully chosen. "To prove to everyone who has doubted him that he's capable of greatness."

Her response was measured and guarded, lacking the depth and sincerity I had come to expect from her. But I chose not to press the issue, sensing that there were layers to Ashlyn's story that she wasn't ready to share.

Instead, I offered her a supportive smile, reaching out to gently squeeze her hand. "I believe in you, Ashlyn," I said softly. "And I know that together, we can make Phantom's racing dreams a reality."

She returned my smile, and I couldn't shake the feeling that there was more to Ashlyn's story than she was letting on.

∼

I found Melody in the barn, her hands busy with the daily care of one of our older horses. I couldn't contain my excitement as I approached her, eager to share the news that had been swirling around in my mind all day. "Hey, Mel," I called out, my voice tinged with anticipation.

Melody turned, a warm smile lighting up her

face as she greeted me. "Hey there, Steph. What's got you all fired up?"

I couldn't help but grin as I launched into an animated explanation. "You won't believe it, but Ashlyn has come up with a plan for Phantom. She wants to enter him in the local derby here in Texas to

see how he copes with race life."

Melody's eyes widened in surprise, a mix of excitement and curiosity flickering in her gaze. "Wow, that's amazing news! Do you think he's ready for something like that?"

I nodded eagerly, my enthusiasm bubbling over. "I think so. Ashlyn has been working with him tirelessly, and he's been responding really well to her training. It's a big step, but I have faith in both of them."

Melody's smile widened, her eyes gleaming with pride. "I'm so happy for you, Stephanie. It sounds like things are really coming together for you and Phantom."

I nodded, pride swelling in my chest. "Yeah, it feels like we're on the right track. And who knows? Maybe this will be the beginning of something truly incredible."

"But what about Ashlyn?" she asked, her brow

furrowing with concern. "Do you trust her completely?"

I paused, a flicker of doubt creeping into my mind as I considered Melody's question. I hesitated, my mind swirling with conflicting thoughts and emotions. "I want to," I admitted, my voice tinged with uncertainty. "But there's something . . . off. I can't quite put my finger on it, but I feel like Ashlyn is hiding something from me."

Melody's expression softened with understanding, her eyes filling with sympathy. "Trust your instincts, Steph," she advised gently. "If something feels wrong, it probably is. But don't jump to conclusions just yet. Maybe there's a good reason she's keeping things from you."

I nodded, grateful for Melody's wisdom and support. "You're right," I conceded, a sense of relief washing over me. "I'll keep an eye on things, but I won't let my worries cloud my judgment. Right now, I need to focus on Phantom, on making sure he's ready for the derby."

Melody nodded in agreement, her smile encouraging. "That's the spirit, Steph. We'll figure this out together, just like we always do."

"All right! Let's get down to business," Melody said, a determined glint in her eye. "The derby's a week away, so we need to make sure everything's in order."

I nodded, feeling a surge of adrenaline at the thought of the upcoming race. "Agreed. First things first. We need to get Phantom registered," I replied, mentally running through the list of tasks

ahead. "Then we'll need to practice loading him into the horsebox. He's been a bit hesitant lately, and we can't afford any hiccups on race day."

Melody nodded in agreement, her expression thoughtful. "And we'll need to schedule a vet check to make sure he's in top form," she added, ticking off items on an imaginary checklist.

I sighed, the weight of responsibility settling on my shoulders. "There's just so much to do," I murmured, feeling a knot of anxiety forming in my stomach. "And that's not even counting the financial aspect. The entry fees, the registration costs, the vet bills, the travel expenses . . . . It's all adding up, Melody."

Melody's brow furrowed with concern as she reached out to squeeze my hand. "I know, Steph. But we'll figure it out together," she reassured me, her voice steady and reassuring. "We've faced tough times before and we've always come out stronger on the other side. We'll find a way to make it work."

Her words were a balm to my frazzled nerves, and I felt gratitude for Melody's friendship wash over me. I knew that we could overcome any obstacle that stood in our way. And as we continued to strategize and plan for the upcoming race, I felt a renewed sense of determination to see it through to the end, no matter what challenges lay ahead.

14

ASHLYN

The morning sun cast a golden glow over the ranch as I led Phantom out of his stall, his powerful frame gleaming in the light. His coat was sleek and glossy, a testament to the hours of grooming and care we had poured into him in preparation for the upcoming derby. As I swung myself into his saddle, I felt a surge of excitement in my veins. Today was another training day, another opportunity to see what Phantom could do on the track.

Phantom moved beneath me with a grace and agility that never failed to impress. His muscles rippled beneath his coat as he pranced eagerly, his hooves striking the ground with a rhythmic cadence that echoed through the quiet morning air. With each movement, I felt a deep connection forming between us—a silent bond that transcended words and language.

As it was still the beginning of our ride, I focused on guiding Phantom through a series of exercises designed to improve his agility and responsiveness. He responded eagerly to my commands, his ears pricked forward in anticipation as we navigated obstacles with precision and skill. With each successful maneuver, I felt so proud. Phantom was not just any horse to me. Instead, he had become a partner, a friend, and a companion on this journey toward greatness.

My choice of training journey for him might be somewhat unusual for a racehorse who is usually sent to the track and knows nothing but the track and his stall, but I liked that Stephanie and I both felt differently than that.

We felt Phantom would be happier if he lived a full and varied life and if he was happier, he would give his best performance on the track. That was the theory anyway.

We picked up speed and Phantom's powerful strides carried us effortlessly across the open expanse of the ranch. I needed to keep his running fitness levels high. I had ridden in races before so I was no stranger to it, but I wouldn't call myself a racing jockey. I had competed (and won at a decent level) in all disciplines over the years from barrel racing and bronc riding- I was an accomplished cowgirl- to the more english equestrian pursuits of Dressage and Eventing. I had started life as a cowgirl so that was always where my heart lay, but I was enamoured with the beauty of horses from the different disciplines. So over the years, I learnt to ride the english way and I spent time with some of the best riders in the world in the different disciplines. I always had a fondness and a skill for the difficult horses. And there always are difficult horses, whatever you are training them for, whether it is racing or dressage.

The wind whipped through my hair as we thundered along, the rush of adrenaline fueling our every move. In that moment, there was nothing else in the world but the two of us.

With each passing moment, I felt more alive, more in tune with Phantom and the world around us. His movements were fluid and graceful, a testament to his natural talent and the countless hours of

training we had put in together. I couldn't help but smile as I felt his power and strength beneath me. He felt strong and fit and I felt happy with the progress we had made. I slowed Phantom to a gentle trot, allowing him to catch his breath. He tossed his head playfully, his eyes shining with intelligence and spirit. In that moment, I knew without a doubt that Phantom although he might have never run a race yet, he was the fastest horse I had ever ridden, and I was grateful for the opportunity to be his partner in this journey.

Then my heart skipped a beat as I saw the horse trailer, a looming presence in the distance. Before I could react, Phantom sensed it too, his muscles tensing beneath me, his ears pinning back in alarm. In an instant, he exploded into action, his powerful hindquarters propelling us forward in a wild burst of speed.

I clung to the reins, fighting to regain control as Phantom bucked and twisted and then bolted, I was entirely unable to slow or stop him. It was the worst situation I've ever been in- the fear of Phantom falling and hurting himself (and probably me) was vivid in my mind as I hauled uselessly at the reins and tried to slow him. The world blurred around us as we raced across the open expanse of the

ranch, the wind whipping past my face in a

dizzying whirl. With each stride, I could feel the fear and panic coursing through Phantom's veins, his instincts urging him to flee from the looming threat. But I refused to let him succumb to his fear. I would let him give in to the chaos unfolding around us.

With all the strength and skill I could muster, I fought to calm Phantom, to soothe his frayed nerves and guide him back to safety. It was a battle of wills and a test of our bond and trust in each other. I

was determined not to let him down.

Slowly, Phantom began to respond to my commands, and he came back to me. With each moment that passed, I felt a sense of relief wash over me, knowing that we were one step closer to overcoming this obstacle together. I headed him back toward the horse trailer at a trot. Finally, with a final nudge from my heels and a reassuring murmur, I guided Phantom to a stop beside the horse trailer. His sides were heaving after the exertion. I dismounted slowly, my legs shaking with adrenaline as I approached him, offering a gentle pat on his neck as a silent reassurance. As I looked into Phantom's eyes, I saw a glimmer of trust and understanding. There was a silent acknowledgment of our bond.

Then my eyes flicked to where Melody and Stephanie stood, their expressions a tumultuous mix of shock, horror, and ultimately, admiration.

For a moment, the weight of their gazes bore down on me and the gravity of what had just happened sunk in. But as Stephanie rushed over, her eyes wide with concern, I felt a surge of relief flood through me. Without hesitation, she enveloped me in a tight hug, her arms a comforting anchor in the midst of chaos.

"I could have lost you," she whispered, her voice thick with emotion. "You handled him so well, Ashlyn. I'm so proud of you." Her words washed over me like a soothing balm, easing the lingering tension in my muscles. I returned her embrace, feeling the warmth of her body pressed against mine.

As Stephanie pulled back, I saw a glimmer of admiration in her eyes, and a silent acknowledgment of the trust she had placed in me, and the faith I had repaid in kind. And in that moment, I knew that our connection ran deeper than mere words could express. Without a second thought, I leaned in and pressed my lips to hers, the taste of victory mingling with relief on our tongues.

Melody's voice cut through the tension like a pop-up ad in the middle of a serious movie scene.

"Well, looks like Phantom just couldn't contain his excitement for the derby," she quipped, her eyes dancing with mischief. Her remark elicited a snort of laughter from Stephanie and me, the absurdity of the situation hitting us like a well-timed punchline. Leave it to Melody to find humor in the midst of something tough, like a comedian crashing a funeral.

Stephanie shot Melody a mock glare, her lips twitching with amusement. "You just couldn't resist, could you?" she teased, her tone fond, despite the lingering tension in the air.

Melody shrugged, a mischievous grin playing at the corners of her lips. "Hey, someone had to break the ice," she replied, her eyes twinkling with mischief. And just like that, the tension dissolved, replaced by a shared sense of amusement.

15

STEPHANIE

The soft light filtered through the window, rousing me from my restless sleep. Pulling me from my dreamless slumber into the hazy realm of early-morning consciousness. My heart beat a steady rhythm of anticipation, the weight of the day's coming events pressing on me like a heavy blanket.

Today was the day, the culmination of weeks of preparation and training. Phantom, my beloved horse, would make his debut on the racing circuit. The thought of it filled me with a heady mix of excitement and apprehension, my stomach knotting with nerves as I contemplated the challenges that lay ahead.

Turning to glance at the clock beside the bed, I

saw that it was barely past five in the morning, the world outside still cloaked in the soft embrace of pre-dawn darkness. The hours stretched out before me, each moment laden with the weight of anticipation. I began to prepare myself mentally for the day ahead.

Beside me, Ashlyn slept on, her breathing steady and even. She was a picture of serenity , in contrast to the turmoil of my racing thoughts. Watching the gentle rise and fall of her chest, I found a momentary respite from the storm raging within me. A fleeting glimpse of tranquility amid the chaos.

With a heavy sigh, I reached out to touch her, my fingers brushing against the warmth of her skin as I traced the contours of her face with feather-light caresses. It was a simple gesture, born of a desire for connection in the quiet stillness of the morning, but it filled me with the sense of calm that I desperately needed during this moment of uncertainty.

I continued to watch her sleep, a wave of affection washing over me, banishing the lingering traces of anxiety that had plagued me since the early hours of the morning. Slumbering in the soft glow of dawn, Ashlyn was like a beacon of light in the darkness. A reminder that no matter what challenges lay ahead, I was not facing them alone. With a soft sigh, I leaned in closer, pressing a fleeting kiss to her forehead before reluctantly pulling away. I felt a soft stirring beside me, the warmth of her presence drawing me closer even as I reluctantly pulled away. Before I could fully retreat, Ashlyn's lips meet mine in a tender kiss. A silent gesture of reassurance that sent a shiver of comfort coursing through me.

In that moment, as Ashlyn held me close, I felt a profound sense of appreciation for the strength and resilience she had brought into my life. Her touch had been a lifeline, grounding me in the here and now. Reminding me that I was not alone in facing the uncertainties that lay ahead.

"It's going to be okay," she whispered against my lips, her voice a gentle murmur that soothed the anxieties swirling within me. "Both Phantom and I are ready for this, Stephanie." Her words helped ease the knot of tension that had settled in the pit of my stomach. With Ashlyn's unwavering support, I felt a renewed sense of determination welling up within me. A quiet resolve that we would face whatever challenges might come our way. She held me close and I drew strength from her presence, finding solace in the warmth of her embrace. With a grateful sigh, I leaned into Ashlyn's touch, savoring the comfort and reassurance she offered.

∽

I drove my old Bronco down the winding country roads, the familiar hum of its engine providing a comforting backdrop to the whirlwind of emotions swirling within me. Alone with my thoughts, I welcomed the solitude, using the quiet drive to piece together the fragments of my scattered mind.

Nervous anticipation gnawed at my insides, creating a tangle of anxiety and excitement as I contemplated the day ahead. The prospect of being surrounded by so many people, each with their own expectations and judgments, sent a shiver of apprehension down my spine. Despite my years in the army, the memories of past traumas still lingered, casting a shadow of doubt over my confidence.

But it wasn't just my own fears that weighed heavily on my mind. As I glanced in the rearview mirror, I saw the horse trailer behind me, carrying Ashlyn and Phantom to the race. The thought of

Phantom, my beloved companion, facing the unknown filled me with unease. I

prayed that he would remain calm and collected, and that he wouldn't succumb to the chaos and confusion of the crowded event.

And then there was Ashlyn. My heart ached with a mixture of longing and concern as I thought of her, riding alongside Phantom in the horse trailer. I knew she was capable, strong and confident, but the

nagging voice of doubt whispered in the back of my mind, taunting me with the possibility of disaster.

I wanted to believe that everything would be okay, that Ashlyn and Phantom would emerge victorious, but the fear of the unknown lingered like a dark cloud on the horizon. With each passing mile, I clung to the hope that somehow, against all odds, we would emerge unscathed from the trials that lay ahead.

∽

As I arrived at the local derby race event, a wave of energy washed over me. The air was electric with excitement and anticipation, while the sprawling grounds were alive with activity. People and horses milled around, their voices mingling in a cacophony of chatter and laughter.

The atmosphere was charged with a sense of camaraderie and competition, as riders and spectators alike gathered to witness the thrilling spectacle unfold before them. Brightly colored tents lined the perimeter of the racetrack, offering an array of refreshments and merchandise to eager betters.

And the racetrack itself was a sight to behold, a sweeping expanse of emerald green stretching out before me, bordered by rows of wooden fencing and adorned with colorful banners fluttering in the breeze. The scent of freshly cut grass mingled with the aroma of hot dogs and popcorn, creating a sensory symphony that enveloped me in a warm embrace.

As I made my way through the crowd, I could feel the rising energy. An excitement that crackled in the air like static electricity. Spectators lined the grandstands, their cheers and applause echoing off the walls as the first race of the day was set up. Everywhere I looked, I saw the glint of leather and the gleam of sleek coats as horses and jockeys prepared for their moment in the spotlight. The tension was a palpable, tangible force that hung heavy in the air. Competitors steeled themselves for the upcoming challenges.

Despite my nerves, there was a sense of exhilaration coursing through my veins. A thrill of anticipation that quickened my pulse and set my heart racing. As I took in the sights and bustling sounds of the event, I couldn't help but feel a surge of pride at being a part of something so vibrant and alive.

I approached Ashlyn and Phantom with a mixture of pride and anxiety. Ashlyn wore the regulation white breeches and boots along with the Blue Jockey silks I had chosen and ordered. A beautiful azure like the sky above our ranch. She looked so very different to the day to day cowgirl Ashlyn. Ashlyn was busy checking Phantom's tack, her focus unwavering as she prepared him for the race ahead. I waited patiently for a moment, allowing her to finish her preparations before gently reaching out to touch her arm.

"Good luck out there," I said softly, my voice tinged with emotion. Ashlyn turned to me, her eyes meeting mine with a mixture of determination and gratitude. Without a word, she leaned in, pressing a tender kiss to my lips before turning back to Phantom, her resolve renewed. She stood facing his tiny racing saddle and looked to me for a second raising her right foot. I went immediately to leg her up onto Phantom as I had so many times before and she flew up as light and graceful as ever and swung her right leg over his back. They were ready to head down to the start. I glanced at them one more time before turning away, my footsteps carrying me towards the owners' section of the grandstand. I took my seat among the other spectators, feeling the heavy weight of anticipation. From my new vantage point, I had a clear view of the racetrack below, and the horses and riders moving gracefully across the lush, green grass. The air was alive with excitement, the crowd buzzing with anticipation for the first race of the day.

I watched anxiously as Ashlyn and Phantom took their position at the start, Phantom so far cooperating and ready for the challenge ahead. He seemed unphased really by everything around him. The other horses, the noise, the crowd. As though all my fears had been for nothing. As though he was born to do this. My heart pounded as the starting bell rang.

16

ASHLYN

Phantom and I were in position- he had walked easily into his stall in the starting gates and I was grateful for that. I could feel the tension coiling in his muscles. We had practiced starts at home so many times- it can be as stressful time for horses.

The air was charge, the roar of the crowd echoing in my ears as we awaited the starting bell. I stole a glance at the other horses, their sleek bodies quivering with excitement. Their riders poised and ready for the race ahead.

The sun beat down on us, enveloping the racetrack in a warm glow. We prepared to embark on our journey. I took a deep breath, trying to calm the butterflies that fluttered in my stomach, reminding myself to trust in Phantom's abilities and in our bond as we faced this challenge together.

When the starting bell finally rang, signaling the beginning of the race and the gates opened, Phantom surged forward with a powerful burst of speed leaping out of the starting gates. His hooves pounded the ground beneath us, kicking up clouds of dust as we tore down the track, the wind at my face.

But as we approached the first corner, Phantom stumbled slightly, throwing us off balance and causing us to fall behind the pack. Panic threatened to overwhelm me as I felt him falter beneath me. I stayed calm and he regained his big strong stride.

I tightened my grip on the reins, my fingers curling around the leather as I urged Phantom onward with firm, yet gentle commands. I could feel his frustration mirroring my own, his muscles tense beneath me as he fought to keep ground with the other horses. With each stride, we gained ground, our pace quickening as we charged around the track. We were passing other horses now. The sound of our hoofbeats echoed in my ears, a steady rhythm that drove us forward with renewed determination.

The wind whipped past us, stinging my cheeks as we thundered down the straightaways. Phantom's powerful strides carried us closer and closer to the front of the pack. I could feel the heat of his

body beneath me, his breath coming in hot bursts as we pushed ourselves to the limit. As we approached the final stretch, I could see the finish line looming ahead. The cheering crowd urged us on and I asked for more from Phantom. The taste of victory was tantalizingly close, spurring us forward with every ounce of strength we possessed.

With a burst of speed in response, Phantom surged forward again, his hooves pounding against the ground as we stormed up the finishing straight. I could feel his muscles straining beneath me, his determination driving us forward with unwavering resolve. And then, in a flurry of motion, we crossed the finish line, the crowd erupting into cheers as we claimed second place. Exhilaration washed over me as I realized what we had accomplished, and Phantom's triumphant neigh echoed in my ears. We had won. A pretty easy win for Phantom's first race. I had known he was special. And I knew in that win he hadn't given all he had to give. He had more speed there that I would keep under wraps for when we really needed it.

We basked in the glory of our victory.

As our placement was announced over the loudspeaker, the crowd's chatter filled the air, a cacophony of voices swirling around me. I could feel their curious gazes on us, their whispers and murmurs blending together in a dizzying haze.

But I couldn't focus on any of it. My mind was still consumed by the rush of adrenaline coursing through my veins. The exhilaration of our victory tingled in every fiber of my being. All I could think about was the bond between Phantom and me. The undeniable connection that had propelled us to success on the racetrack.

I lead Phantom off to weigh out and get washed down, showering him with praise and affection, running my hands over his sleek black coat while whispering words of encouragement in his ear. He nuzzled against me, his warm breath tickling my skin as we reveled in the moment together.

The crowd's chatter faded into the background

as I focused all my attention on Phantom, the world melting away as we shared a quiet moment of celebration.

Stephanie and Melody spotted us as we headed towards the unsaddling area, their faces lit up with joy and pride. They rushed over to us, their excitement palpable as they congratulated us on our incredible performance. Stephanie wrapped me in a tight hug, her warmth and affection washing over me like a comforting embrace.

I wanted her to never let go.

"You did it, Ashlyn," she said, her voice filled with pride. "I knew you two could do it."

Melody joined the celebration, clapping her hands and cheering loudly. "That was amazing!" she exclaimed, her eyes shining with admiration. "You and Phantom make quite the team."

I couldn't help but smile at their enthusiasm, feeling a sense of camaraderie and belonging wash over me. In this moment, surrounded by my friends and colleagues, I felt like I was exactly where I was supposed to be.

I pulled Stephanie close, savoring the sweetness of our shared victory.

Then, I caught a glimpse of someone in the crowd. For a fleeting moment, my heart skipped a beat. I could have sworn that I saw a familiar face, a young woman. Someone from my past at Brooks Creek.

My grip tightened around Stephanie as a surge of unease washed over me. Could it be her? Could she have followed me here, to this small Texas town? But then I shook my head, chiding myself for being paranoid. It had been ages since I left Brooks Creek, and surely she wouldn't have come all this way just to find me. As quickly as the fear arose, I pushed it down, burying it beneath a facade of celebration. I couldn't let my past haunt me, not now. Not when we were celebrating this momentous occasion. Feeling Stephanie's warmth beside me, I forced a smile, dismissing the nagging doubts that lingered in the back of my mind.

Instead, I wrapped my arm around Stephanie, pulling her close and pressing my lips to hers in a fervent kiss. In that embrace, I found solace and reassurance. My mind still raced, flickering with paranoia, but I forced myself to stay in the moment. This was supposed to be a celebration, a moment of triumph for us both. I couldn't let my past cast a shadow over our happiness.

Stephanie's laughter rang in my ears, her smile lighting up her face as she pulled away from our kiss, her eyes sparkling with joy. "We did it," she exclaimed, her voice filled with excitement.

"Yeah, we did," I replied, my own voice tinged with relief. But even as I spoke the words, I couldn't shake the feeling of unease that lingered in the depths of my mind. As we basked in the afterglow of our victory, I made a silent promise to myself: I wouldn't let my past dictate my future. I would face whatever challenges lay ahead with courage and determination, knowing that as long as I had Stephanie by my side, we could overcome anything together.

With that thought in mind, I turned my attention back to the celebration, determined to savor every moment of this joyous occasion. And as the cheers of the crowd echoed around us, I found myself smiling, the fear and doubt slowly fading away in the warmth of Stephanie's embrace.

∽

As Melody nodded and started to load Phantom into the trailer, I turned toward Stephanie's Bronco, a smirk playing at the corners of my lips. "Well now, darlin'," I drawled in my best fake

Southern accent, "you reckon there's room for two in that there truck of yours?"

Stephanie chuckled, her eyes sparkling with amusement as she opened the passenger door. "I reckon we can make some room," she replied, her own accent slipping into a Texan twang. I slid into the truck beside her, the familiar scent of leather and hay enveloping me as I settled into the worn seat. The engine rumbled to life beneath us, the sound comforting in its familiarity as Stephanie pulled away from the race track.

We drove along and the tension of the day began to melt away, and was soon replaced by a sense of contentment and ease. Stephanie's presence beside me was like a warm blanket, soothing and reassuring as we made our way back to the ranch. We chatted idly as we drove, sharing stories and laughter, the miles passing by in a blur of scenery and conversation. It was moments like those, simple and unassuming, that I treasured the most—the quiet moments with Stephanie, free from the chaos and uncertainty of the outside world.

"So, what happens now with Phantom?" Stephanie asked, breaking the silence as we drove. "What's the plan?"

I glanced over at her, a smile tugging at the corners of my lips as I reached over to gently brush my fingers against hers. "Well, first things first. We'll need to get him settled back at the ranch," I replied,

my voice soft. "Then we'll start working on his training regimen, getting him ready for the next race."

Stephanie nodded, her gaze fixed on the road ahead as she listened intently. "And what about you?" she asked, her voice laced with curiosity. "What's next for Ashlyn Beech?"

I took a moment to consider her question, my thoughts drifting to the future. "Honestly, I'm not sure," I admitted, my fingers tracing idle patterns on the fabric of her jeans. "But for now, I'm just happy to be here, with you."

Stephanie's smile softened. Her hand found mine and gave it a reassuring squeeze. "I'm happy you're here too, Ashlyn," she murmured, her voice barely above a whisper. "I'm happy you're here

too."

My fingers continued to trace gentle patterns along Stephanie's thigh, and I felt the tension between us building with each passing moment.

The warmth of her skin beneath my touch sent a shiver

down my spine, igniting a fire that burned with a fierce intensity. Leaning closer to her, I felt the electricity crackling between us, the air thick with anticipation. Our eyes locked in a shared moment of silent understanding, the world around us fading into the background as we become lost in each other's gaze.

Suddenly, Stephanie spotted a secluded place by the side of the road, the perfect place to pull over and steal a moment alone together. With a quick glance, she guided the truck to the side of the road, the engine rumbling to a halt as we came to a stop.

Turning to face her, I found myself lost in the depths of her gaze, the desire in her eyes mirroring my own. Without a word, I closed the distance between us, capturing her lips in a searing kiss that left us both breathless and wanting more. Time seemed to stand still as we lost ourselves in the heat of the moment, the world around us fading away. Our kiss deepened, the tension between us reaching its peak as we gave in to the desire that had been building between us all day.

"You were incredible." Stephanie's words

washed over me like a warm embrace, her praise filling me with pride and satisfaction.

Breaking away from the kiss, I gazed into Stephanie's eyes, emotion welling up inside me. "I did it for you," I whispered as I caressed her cheek with the back of my hand.

My hand reached down, sliding between her knees and then pushing further up between her lovely thighs under her skirt.

Her moan was a clear encouragement as she tipped her head back and parted her legs to allow me access and before I knew it, the lace of her panties was in my hand. I pressed against it and felt her wetness even through the panties. I played around them, toyed with the now damp fabric between my fingers, enjoying every second of her moans and shudders as my fingers teased her.

I watched as her nipples hardened beneath the thin fabric of her dress. Pleasing Stephanie was always such a pleasure for me. Watching her enjoy my touch drove me crazy. I felt my own desire pulsing in my jeans.

I pulled her panties to the side and gave her more direct contact and I thought for a second she might jump off the seat with excitement. Her body responded and she felt wetter and I adjusted my position as best as I could within the confines of the truck, leaning across as best as possible so I could angle my wrist. She didn't need asking to shift her hips forwards to allow me access, she did it instinctively. We were always in tune sexually, as though our bodies were made to make music together.

My fingers pushed into her deeply and firmly.

"Oh, god... oh... Ash..." she cried out as I began to fuck her deeply and slowly to start with, my fingers curled up to her G spot, teasing at her clitoris with my thumb as I went.

She raised her hips to move with me and she met me with hips that wanted more.

I felt so high from the events of the day, sex is always something I like following winning and this was no different.

Except, it was actually different. Sex with Stephanie was actually always different because I felt something beyond pure lust. I felt pure lust for her, of course. But I also felt a connection. An other worldly connection as though our souls were meant to be joined.

I added another finger and increased the tempo of my thrusts. Of course it wasn't easy in a vehicle, but I wanted her so badly and it couldn't wait.

"You are amazing," I whispered to her and she opened her eyes for a second, her eyes glinting navy blue in the dark. "So beautiful," I said and we connected and were still for just a second, my fingers so deep inside of her. I could feel her body pulsing around my fingers.

"I love you," she whispered, her eyes glazed with lust.

"I love you, too, " I smiled at her and held her like that for just another few seconds longer as I kissed her lips, tenderly.

"I'm going to make you come so hard all over the seat of this Bronco," I said, wickedness in my voice and we both laughed.

"Go on then," she challenged and I went back to work, thrusting into her harder, faster, just how I knew she wanted it.

Her breathing quickened and her cheeks flushed in the dark and I knew she was close, very close.

"Come for me, my darling," I said and it took only those words to tip her over the edge as her orgasm overtook her and I felt her body go rigid before relaxing into post orgasmic bliss. I felt the wetness of her orgasm in the palm of my hand.

God, it was always so satisfying, fucking her.

I felt a sense of deep satisfaction within me as she came back to life and smiled warmly at me.

"You are so good at that," she said. "Well, I know you know that. I don't know why I am telling you, but you are."

I smiled. It wasn't the first compliment my sexual skills had had but it was the first time it meant so much more, coming from her lips. I started to think that maybe I could be the woman she needed me to be. With her, maybe things would be different.

A car drove past, its headlights casting fleeting shadows across our faces, and we broke apart with a shared giggle. Our laughter mingled with the gentle rustle of the evening breeze. Despite the interruption, the warmth of Stephanie's hand in mine filled me with a sense of contentment as we continued our journey back home.

Stephanie drove and I leaned back in my seat, my hand intertwined with hers, feeling a sense of calm wash over me. The soft hum of the engine had lulled me into a state of tranquility as she navigated the familiar roads that led back to the ranch. Our conversation flowed effortlessly, filled with laughter and shared memories. Stephanie's presence was a comforting anchor, grounding me in the moment and

banishing any lingering doubts or fears. With each passing mile, our connection deepened. Our hands remained entwined as we moved through the twists and turns together. In that moment, there was only Stephanie and me, our bond growing stronger with each passing moment.

Eventually, we pulled into the ranch, the moon dipping just above the horizon in a blaze of bright white and gold. Stephanie cut the engine and we sat in comfortable silence for a moment, savoring the peace of the evening. "Thanks for the ride," I say softly, breaking the quiet.

Stephanie smiles, her eyes soft and warm in the fading light. "Anytime, Ashlyn," she replied, her voice gentle and reassuring. "Anytime."

∼

Later that night, I was naked and bathed and in Stephanie's bed and Stephanie got out the bath and padded naked across the floor to me.

She look ethereal in the dim golden lamplight.

Her skin and hair shone golden and I thought again how beautiful she was.

She didn't speak, she just pulled back the comforter and made her way between my legs on her knees, parting my legs as she went and she smiled at me just before she dipped her head to my pussy to please me.

I felt her tongue move in long slow strokes as though enjoying me, as though savouring every moment and I felt myself relaxing entirely, my head back on the pillow and my legs parting further to give her easier access.

Her mouth was leisurely in its pleasuring of me. As though we had all night. (and we did.)

I enjoyed it in a way I can't remember ever enjoying sex before. I was enjoying the feelings and the sensations rather than chasing a climax as fast as I can.

My hips moved with her head pressing forwards, pulling back. Her tongue, long firm strokes, then gentle licks. We danced together with her head between my legs taking me to places I had never been.

Things built and built slowly in a way that I never saw coming. When my orgasm did tear through me it was in a way I have never felt before.

More intense than anything I could ever have imagined and I felt it in every single part of me that thrummed and buzzed with the thrill of it.

When I opened my eyes, she was lying on top of me, her face inches from my own. I felt tears in my own eyes, I was crying. She kissed my face, kissing each of my tears away and when she kissed my mouth I tasted my sex and my pain on her tongue.

17

STEPHANIE

I sat at the rustic wooden table in the kitchen, sipping my morning coffee and daydreaming about our sex and the familiar sound of the mailbox creaking open outside caught my attention. Wondering what had arrived, I stepped out

onto the porch and retrieved the small stack of letters and bills. I flipped through them absent-mindedly.

One envelope caught my eye—a letter from the bank, its official seal staring back at

me. With a furrowed brow, I tore it open, my heart pounding with a mix of apprehension and uncertainty.

Reading through the contents of the letter, my

heart sank. It was a notice from the bank, informing me that I needed to come in for a meeting about my financial status. My mind raced with worry about the ranch's expenses. I knew the truth—I had poured my heart and soul into this ranch, using every penny of my savings and army discharge money to purchase it. I had managed to escape without needing a mortgage. But the cost of running the farm, coupled with the expenses of caring not only for the other animals, but for Ashlyn, Melody and Phantom, had begun to take its toll on my finances.

I felt anxious and uncertain about what the meeting would entail. Would I be able to secure the funds needed to keep the ranch afloat, or would I be forced to make a difficult decision about its future?

As I sat at the kitchen table, lost in my thoughts, the sound of footsteps drew me out of my reverie. Melody entered, her expression soft with concern as she saw me sitting there, the letter from the bank still clutched in my hand.

"Hey, Steph, everything all right?" Melody's voice was gentle, her eyes filled with genuine concern as she came over.

I offered her a weak smile, trying to push aside

the waves of worry that threatened to overwhelm me. "Yeah, just got some news from the bank. Looks like I need to go in for a meeting about my finances."

Melody's brow furrowed in understanding and she took a seat across from me, her presence a comforting anchor. "Is it serious?"

I sighed, uncertainty settling in the pit of my stomach. "I'm not sure yet. But the ranch expenses have been adding up and I know I need to figure out a way to keep everything afloat."

Melody reached out, placing a reassuring hand on mine. "You're not alone in this, Steph. We'll figure it out."

Her words eased my frazzled nerves and I offered her a grateful smile. "Thanks, Mel. I appreciate it more than you know."

Ashlyn came down the stairs just then, her presence adding a flicker of warmth to the room, but I didn't want to burden her with my worries. She approached us, concern etched on her features as she glanced between Melody and me. "Hey, is everything all right?" Ashlyn's voice was soft and her eyes searched mine for signs of distress.

I hesitated, unsure how to broach the subject.

But before I could find the words, Melody stepped in, her tone gentle, but firm. "We just got some news from the bank, Ash. Stephanie needs to go in for a meeting about the ranch's finances," Melody explained, her gaze steady as she met Ashlyn's eyes.

Ashlyn's brow furrowed with concern. She moved closer, her hand finding mine in a comforting gesture. "Is it serious?"

I swallowed hard, feeling the weight of the situation. "I'm not sure yet. But money's been tight lately and I know I need to figure out a way to make ends meet."

Ashlyn's expression softened with understanding and she squeezed my hand reassuringly.

∼

As I drove to the bank, I suddenly realized that I felt completely exhausted. My old Bronco rattled down the road, the familiar hum of the engine doing little to calm my racing thoughts. I glanced down at my outfit—a crisp, white button-down shirt tucked into high-waisted trousers. It was the best I had, but as I looked in the rearview mirror, I noticed how worn and faded the fabric had become over time. I used to feel confident in this ensemble and considered it a reflection of my professional demeanor. Now, my outfit made me feel like a shadow of my former self.

I had spent the last few days replaying every financial decision I had made, every expense that had piled up, and every dream I'd had for the ranch. The memories of laughter shared with Ashlyn, the thrill of Phantom's first race, and the comforting routine of caring for the animals all seemed distant now, overshadowed by the impending doom of the upcoming meeting.

I pulled into the bank's parking lot, took a deep breath, and steadied myself for what lay ahead.

The building loomed before me, in stark contrast to the freedom of the ranch. This place felt suffocating, its sterile walls a reminder of the financial shackles I was about to face. I stepped out of the Bronco, gravel crunching beneath my boots as I approached the entrance.

Inside, the air was cool, a welcome reprieve from the Texas heat, but it did nothing to ease the anxiety swirling in my gut. I had always found comfort in the chaos of the ranch, the symphony of horse whinnies and clucking hens, but now I was stepping into a world that felt foreign and intimidating.

"Good morning, Stephanie!" Bill's voice boomed from behind the reception desk as I entered. His warmth was immediate and I appreciated the way his eyes crinkled with genuine delight upon

seeing me. Bill was a big man, with a heart to match, and I knew he had a soft spot for ranchers and their dreams.

"Morning, Bill," I replied, forcing a smile as I made my way to his office. The familiar scent of coffee lingered in the air, mingling with the faint aroma of horse leather that he seemed to carry with him.

As I settled into the chair across from his desk, I couldn't help but notice the framed pictures of horses that adorned the walls—each one a testament to his passion. "So, how's Phantom doing?" he asked, leaning back in his chair, his expression curious yet concerned.

"He's doing great. Ashlyn's really bringing out the best in him," I said, my pride in Phantom's progress surfacing, despite the weight of the conversation looming over us.

"That's fantastic to hear!" Bill's enthusiasm was

genuine and it made me feel a glimmer of hope. But as I looked into his eyes, I could see his underlying concern. "Now, let's talk about the ranch."

I took a deep breath, preparing myself to lay bare my vulnerabilities. "I've been struggling to keep up with the costs lately. I know I've taken out loans and I'm worried about falling behind on them."

Bill nodded, his expression serious as he shuffled through some papers on his desk. "I understand, and I want to help you. But we need to figure out a sustainable plan to get you back on track. The

expenses have been rising and I'm concerned about your ability to keep the ranch afloat."

His words hit me like a punch to the gut and I felt my chest tighten. I knew he was right, but I couldn't let the ranch—my sanctuary—slip through my fingers. "I'm willing to do whatever it takes," I

said, my voice steady despite the storm raging inside me.

Bill leaned forward, his eyes searching mine. "That's the spirit, Stephanie. But we need to be realistic. Have you considered cutting back on some of the expenses?"

I nodded, my mind racing with potential solutions. "I'm open to it. I just need to find a way to keep the ranch running, while also taking care of Phantom and the other animals."

Bill sighed, his expression softening. "You're passionate about this and I want to see you succeed. But we need a solid plan moving forward."

I sat there, feeling the enormity of the situation settle over me. This wasn't just about finances. It was about my life, my dreams, and everything I had fought for. But I couldn't let fear dictate my

actions. I was determined to save my ranch, no matter what it took.

Bill leaned back in his chair, studying me closely. I could feel the weight of his gaze, and knew he was assessing my reluctance to discuss any drastic changes. After a moment, he cleared his throat, breaking the silence that had settled over us. "Stephanie," he began, his tone thoughtful. "I've been hearing a lot of buzz about Phantom since that local derby. It seems like he really has potential."

I nodded, feeling a swell of pride at the mention of Phantom's name. "He does. Ashlyn has a real way with him. They've built an incredible bond and it shows on the track."

Bill smiled, the corners of his mouth lifting as he nodded. "That's great to hear. But have you considered entering him in the state race coming up? I've heard the prize is a hundred grand for first place."

My heart raced at the thought. One hundred thousand dollars! That could change everything for the ranch.

"The state race?" I said. "I . . . I hadn't really thought about it. That's a huge commitment."

"I get that," Bill said, leaning forward, his elbows resting on the desk. "But think about what that kind of money could do for you. It could secure the ranch for the next two years, and that would give you a little breathing room. I could defer your debts for the next month until the race, allowing you to focus on preparing Phantom without that added pressure."

I let his words sink in, possibilities swirling in my mind. "You really think he has a chance?" I asked, my voice barely above a whisper.

"From what I've seen and heard, absolutely. And, I am a betting man. But it all depends on how you handle the training and preparation. Ashlyn seems to have a good grasp on him. With the right approach, you could be in it to win."

I felt a mix of excitement and trepidation at the thought. "What if we don't win? What if Phantom isn't ready?" My anxiety crept back in, tightening my chest.

Bill waved a hand dismissively, a reassuring smile on his face. "You won't know unless you try.

You've already seen what he can do in a competitive setting. Just think of the confidence that a win will bring you and Ashlyn. Besides, with the right training regimen, I believe he will be ready."

I closed my eyes for a moment, envisioning Phantom's powerful strides as he thundered down the track, the wind whipping through his mane and Ashlyn's focused determination guiding him. The picture felt exhilarating, yet terrifying. "I know Ashlyn is dedicated, but we're still relatively new to this. The state race is a whole different ball game."

"True," Bill conceded, "but every race is a learning experience. This is an opportunity to elevate both your and Phantom's standing in the racing community. It's your chance to shine and I believe you both can rise to the occasion. You're a talented owner and coach, and with Ashlyn's support, I can't see any reason why you shouldn't take this leap."

A fire ignited within me at his encouragement. "You really think we can do it?"

"Without a doubt," Bill replied, his voice firm. "I've seen you work with Phantom, and I believe in your ability to manage this. Plus, it would secure your financial future for a while. You won't be just surviving; you'll be thriving."

I ran a hand through my hair, the weight of his words settling in. This was a significant decision, but it also felt like a possible turning point. "If we do this, I want to make sure Ashlyn is on board. She's been instrumental in Phantom's training and I don't want to take her for granted."

Bill nodded approvingly. "That's a smart move. You'll need to communicate and strategize together. It's a partnership, after all. But don't forget that this is also about you, Stephanie. You've put in so much hard work. Don't shy away from this opportunity just because you're worried about the 'what ifs.'"

Somewhere in the middle of our meeting, my anxiety had begun to dissipate, to be replaced by a glimmer of hope. "Okay. I'll talk to Ashlyn. If she's up for it, then I think we can make this happen."

"Great!" Bill beamed, his excitement infectious. "I'm here to support you every step of the way.

Let's get Phantom registered and I'll help you set up a training plan. This is the beginning of something big, Stephanie."

"Thank you, Bill. I really appreciate your belief in me. It means a lot," I said, feeling a renewed sense of purpose.

I left his office feeling excited. The upcoming state race could be our chance to turn everything around. Now I just needed to gather the courage to speak with Ashlyn.

18

ASHLYN

The sun was low in the sky, casting a golden hue over the sprawling fields. I rode Phantom along familiar trails. With each rhythmic beat of his hooves, I felt a sense of calm wash over me, as if the world around us had faded away. It was just me and him, a powerful partnership that had developed into something magical over the past few weeks. He moved effortlessly beneath me, his strong muscles working in perfect harmony as we navigated the winding paths of the ranch.

I couldn't help but smile at how far we'd come together. Phantom had transformed from a spirited, somewhat unruly horse into a confident competitor. He was no longer just a beautiful creature; he

was my teammate, my equal in a way I had never anticipated. As we cantered through the fields, I felt a connection with him that transcended words—a bond built on trust and understanding. I could

sense his energy, his excitement, as he galloped forward, eager to explore every inch of the land we called home.

But even in the midst of this blissful ride, my thoughts drifted back to Stephanie and the financial strain she was facing. I knew she was worried about the ranch and the costs of running it. About how the future looked uncertain.

I could help her. I had the means to do so in a heartbeat. I had a considerable amount, money that was meant to provide me with a fresh start—a new life away from the chaos of my past.

But the thought of sharing that wealth with Stephanie brought up a torrent of conflicting emotions.

What would she think if I offered her money? Would she feel embarrassed, or worse, indebted? I couldn't bear the thought of Stephanie looking at me differently. Questioning where the money came from, or why I had it in the first place. There was still a part of me that worried about being discovered. My past life and the secrets I had buried so deep threatened to resurface. The last thing I wanted was to taint what we were building together with my past mistakes.

"Easy there, big guy," I murmured to Phantom, feeling his eagerness beneath me. He pranced forward, clearly picking up on my tension. I gently squeezed my legs, urging him to slow down. He complied, settling into a steady trot as I took a deep breath, trying to shake off my worries.

The crisp air filled my lungs and I focused on the rhythm of his movement, allowing the connection between us to ground me. I remembered the way Phantom had raced around the track, fueled by adrenaline and the thrill of competition. It was during those moments that I realized how much I loved riding him. How much I loved being in control, while letting him shine.

"Let's show them what we're made of," I whispered, patting his neck affectionately. Phantom tossed his head, as if in agreement, and I felt a rush of excitement pulse through me. We had a race coming up soon. While the thought of competition thrilled me, it also made my heart race for entirely different reasons. Would Phantom be ready? Would we be able to stand out from the other competitors?

But then I thought of Stephanie's face, and remembered how proud she had looked after Phantom's first race. She had believed in us when we needed it most, and I wanted to return that faith. I could still see Stephanie standing at the edge of the track, her eyes alight with joy as she cheered us on. I wanted to make her proud, not just as a rider, but as someone who could take care of her own.

We went around a bend in the trail and I leaned down to whisper sweet nothings to Phantom. "We'll figure it out. I promise." He snorted softly and I felt warmth radiating from his body, a reminder that we were in this together.

But the reality of Stephanie's situation still loomed over me like a dark cloud. What if she refused my financial help, even if I offered? What if my wealth only complicated things further? She had always been fiercely independent, a trait I admired, but I could see the cracks beginning to form under the pressure. The last thing I wanted was to push her away by offering too much too soon.

And aside from that, although in some ways we were closer than ever, I was keeping secrets and I knew she was holding something back, too.

We approached a small rise in the landscape and I felt Phantom's muscles tense beneath me, his instincts kicking in as he sensed the change in terrain. I urged him forward, feeling the thrill of adrenaline rush through us as we leapt over the crest. The world spread out before us, a sprawling panorama of green fields and distant hills. For a moment, I forgot my worries. In that instant, I

felt invincible, as if nothing could touch us.

But as we descended and returned to the gentle slope, my doubts returned. I wanted to be open with Stephanie, to share everything with her. I wanted to tell her that I could help, that I could ease some of her burdens. But I hesitated, unsure how to approach the topic. I didn't want to bring it up too soon or make her feel uncomfortable. I wanted Stephanie to know that I cared, but I also wanted her to stand on her own two feet.

Maybe I'll just wait a little longer, I thought, feeling a twinge of guilt. *She'll ask if she needs it. She always has.* But I couldn't shake the feeling that if I didn't say something soon, this might become a barrier between us—a wall built from unspoken words and hidden truths.

With a sigh, I nudged Phantom into a gallop, the wind whipping through my hair. And I let go of my worries, if only for a moment. The horse responded eagerly, charging ahead, and I focused on the rhythm of his movements, the beat of his heart matching my own. In that beautiful moment, I knew we were unstoppable together. I could only hope that our bond could withstand the pressures of

our current reality.

∼

I led Phantom into the barn, the familiar scent of hay and leather wrapping around me like a warm embrace. The soft nickers of the other horses soothed me as I carefully unfastened his saddle, the day's adrenaline still buzzing through my veins. I felt a rush of satisfaction at how well Phantom been today, but my exhilaration was tempered by an underlying tension that had started to gnaw at my insides.

Just as I finished brushing down Phantom, I heard the unmistakable sound of footsteps approaching. I turned, my heart fluttering as I saw Stephanie step into the dim light of the barn.

Her face was alight with excitement and her eyes were sparkling as she rushed towards me.

"Ashlyn!" she exclaimed, her voice ringing with enthusiasm. "You won't believe what I just talked about with Bill! He thinks Phantom has real potential. If you win the state race in two weeks, we can secure everything! He's confident we can make it work!"

My stomach dropped as her words sank in. The weight of her expectations felt heavy. I forced a smile, but inside, my mind was racing. Winning that race was not just a challenge; it was a direct violation of the agreement I had signed.

"Stephanie, I—" I started, but she didn't seem to notice the hesitation in my voice.

"I mean it, Ashlyn! You were incredible, and I just know you can rise to the occasion again! I have complete faith in you. We can turn this around!" Her excitement was infectious, yet I felt a dark cloud forming over my heart.

"Stephanie, wait," I said, trying to keep my tone steady. "You don't understand. Competing in that race . . . it's complicated."

She stopped, her brow furrowing as she

searched my face for answers. "What do you mean? You have to see this as a chance! We can save the ranch!"

"I know that, but . . . " My voice faltered, the words I needed to say catching in my throat. "I can't just enter any race. There are consequences. They're—"

"Consequences?" she interrupted, her voice rising slightly, frustration creeping into her tone.

"Ashlyn, this is our chance! We can't just throw it away because of some old doubt. You're incredible on that horse, and you know it! You can't let anything hold you back!"

"Don't you see?" I snapped, anger bubbling up inside me. "It's not that simple!"

Her expression shifted from excitement to confusion, and I felt the hurt in her eyes as Stephanie took a step back, the reality of my words sinking in. "I thought you wanted to help us," she said quietly,

disappointment lacing her tone.

"I do want to help you! I want to save the ranch! But not like this," I replied, my voice softer now, anger giving way to fear. "If I race and something goes wrong, I could lose everything. You could lose everything." Silence hung between us, thick and heavy. I could see the gears turning in Stephanie's head as she processed what I was saying.

"But we've come so far, Ashlyn! I believed in you. I thought we were in this together," she said, her voice trembling slightly. "You're so talented, and I thought we could face this together."

"We can, but not like this," I insisted, my heart aching.

Her eyes narrowed, hurt etched on her face. "So what? You're just going to walk away? You're going to throw in the towel because you're scared?"

"No! I'm trying to protect us! I want to be here for you and for Phantom."

"Then what do you want me to do?" she asked, her voice breaking slightly. "Just give up? Let everything fall apart because you're afraid?"

I took a deep breath, feeling the anger dissipate, leaving only vulnerability in its wake. "I want you to understand where I'm coming from. I want you to trust that I'm trying to do what's best for both of us. I thought we were building something real together, but if this is what it's going to take..."

"It's not just a race, Ashlyn! It's our future! Can't you see that?" Her voice was louder now, her frustration boiling over. "I can't believe you're willing to just let it go!"

I could feel my own frustration creeping back, a battle of emotions raging within me. "I'm not letting it go! I'm trying to figure out how to move forward without jeopardizing everything!"

"Then help me understand! Talk to me!" she pleaded, her eyes searching mine for a connection, an answer.

I stood there, feeling the turmoil churning inside me. I had never been one to shy away from a challenge, yet this felt different. It felt dangerous. But the alternative—losing Stephanie, losing everything we had built together—was far worse. I took a deep breath, my heart racing as I realized what I had to do.

"Okay," I said, my voice steadier than I felt. "I'll do it. I'll race at the state event."

The relief that flooded her features was immediate, and I couldn't help but feel a pang of guilt.

"Really? You'll do it?" she asked, her eyes lighting up with hope. "I knew you could! You were amazing out there, and we'll prepare just like we did for the local derby."

"Yeah, I just . . . I was nervous," I added, trying to deflect her enthusiasm away from the truth. I didn't want to admit that my nerves were rooted in my fear of being discovered. Fear of my past crashing into my present like a runaway train.

"Nervous? You? That's hard to believe," she teased, a smile creeping onto her face. "I mean, you practically made Phantom fly!"

I chuckled softly, appreciating her attempt to lighten the mood. "Well, maybe it was more about getting the hang of riding him. He's got some serious speed."

"Exactly! And together, you two are unstoppable," she said, her voice bubbling with excitement. But even as she spoke, I noticed the flicker of doubt behind her eyes, as if she sensed I wasn't being entirely truthful. I steeled myself against it, knowing that I had to keep my past hidden.

"Listen, we have two weeks to get him in top shape," she continued, the determination in her voice palpable. "We'll do everything we can to make sure he's ready for the race. I'll help however I can—training, feeding, whatever it takes."

"Thanks, Stephanie. I appreciate that." My fingers brushed against hers, a fleeting moment of connection that sent warmth through me, although the undercurrent of tension remained. "We'll figure it out together."

The conversation shifted back to training schedules and strategies, and as we discussed everything from workouts to nutrition for Phantom, I could feel my anxiety starting to ebb away, replaced by a sense of purpose. But in the back of my mind, the nagging thought of the contract loomed large. I couldn't let Stephanie see how afraid I really was. I had to protect her, even if it meant putting myself in a risky position.

"Okay, so what's the plan for the next few days?" I asked, trying to refocus. "We need to get Phantom acclimated to race day conditions. Maybe we should get him used to the noise and crowds."

"Absolutely! We can take him to the local fair next weekend. They'll have music, people, and everything. It'll be perfect practice." She grinned, her enthusiasm infectious, and I couldn't help but smile back, even as the situation seemed heavier on my shoulders.

As we continued talking, planning every detail for Phantom's training, I felt a shift in our dynamic. It wasn't just about the race anymore. It was about our future together. I wanted to keep Stephanie safe and I wanted to be there for her. But I couldn't shake my anxiety that this all hinged on me. If I failed, it wouldn't just be my loss—it would be hers too.

"Are you sure you're okay, Ashlyn?" she asked again, her eyes searching mine, and I felt a pang of guilt about the way I was deflecting her concern.

"I'm fine, really," I assured her, though the words felt hollow in my throat. "Just trying to take it all in. This is a big deal."

Stephanie studied me a moment longer and I could feel her instincts kicking in. I knew she was smart and I hated the idea of lying to her. "Okay, but if you ever want to talk, I'm here," she said softly, her voice full of sincerity. I nodded, grateful for her support, but I also felt the chasm grow wider between us. How could I ever explain my past without risking everything? I couldn't let her know about the agreement I'd made—the one that had kept me shackled to my old life.

"I'll be ready," I finally said, forcing a confident smile. "We'll make this happen."

With that, I reached out and took Stephanie's hand in mine, intertwining our fingers. For a moment, it felt like everything would be okay. But beneath the surface, the storm raged on, and I knew that in two weeks, everything would come to a head.

We left the barn as the sun dipped low on the horizon I took a deep breath, steeling myself for the challenges ahead. I would race in the state competition—not just for Phantom and the ranch, but also for Stephanie. She believed in me and I had to find a way to make her dreams a reality, even if it meant confronting my own demons along the way.

19

STEPHANIE

I watched Ashlyn's face and the myriad of emotions that danced across her features, revealing a struggle that tugged at my heart. Despite her bravado, I could sense her underlying tension. I could tell by the way her fingers fidgeted and her gaze flitted to the side, as if searching for an escape. There was something Ashlyn wasn't telling me, something that curled around my gut like a snake. While my instinct urged me to pursue the truth, to demand she open up to me completely, I hesitated.

The reality of our situation loomed larger than any hidden secret. The race in two weeks wasn't just a competition; it was my lifeline. The responsibility was intense. If Phantom was going to secure our future, then all of my energy and focus needed to be directed toward that goal. But how could I do that while knowing Ashlyn was holding back?

I took a deep breath, reminding myself that I had to trust her abilities. She was exceptional with Phantom—a natural rider whose confidence radiated from her. The bond the two of them shared was undeniable, and maybe that was enough.

I had to channel my anxiety into a fierce determination for the raceahead. The financial strain and the fear of losing the ranch—those were battles for another day. "Okay," I said, my voice steady. "We'll focus on the race. I believe in you, Ashlyn. I know you can win."

As soon as the words left my mouth, I felt a surge of conviction. I would throw myself into this challenge alongside her, pushing aside my worries about whatever Ashlyn was hiding.

Her face softened in response, a hint of gratitude flickering in her eyes. "Thank you, Stephanie. It means everything to me that you believe in us." There was something in her voice that made my heart skip. It was more than just gratitude; it was a thread of connection that pulled me closer to her. The way Ashlyn looked at me, the warmth in her gaze—it made my insides flutter. I wanted to reach out, to hold her, and to erase the distance that had crept between us. The love I felt for her was undeniable, an undercurrent that surged with every shared moment.

But I had to be strong. "We'll work together to prepare Phantom for the race," I said, forcing myself voice to be steady. "We'll get him in shape, practice our strategies, and make sure he's ready to go."

"Absolutely," she agreed, her tone shifting to that of a determined partner. "I'll spend extra time with him too, working on stamina and speed. I know he's got it in him."

"Together, we'll make this happen," I replied, feeling a spark of hope ignite within me. "I'll help however I can."

As I looked at Ashlyn, at the way her hair caught the light and the softness of her expression, I felt a rush of affection. But it was overshadowed by a sense of urgency. The race was our immediate

concern, but the unresolved tension between us loomed large. Whatever Ashlyn was hiding felt like a chasm that could open up at any moment. I knew I had to navigate it carefully.

"Let's get to work then," I said, forcing a smile even as uncertainty gnawed at me. "We'll train hard and win this race. And after that . . . " My voice trailed off as I considered the next steps. The

impending confrontation with whatever truth lay between us. But for now, I had to keep my focus on the task at hand.

With a deep breath, I took a step toward her, brushing my fingers lightly against Ashlyn's arm. The connection sparked like electricity, sending a shiver through me. In that moment, the world outside

faded away. It was just us, two women standing on the precipice of something powerful. But would our connection be enough to withstand whatever storm was brewing just beyond our horizon?

∼

I moved through the quiet kitchen. The world outside was still cloaked in darkness. I reached for the coffee pot and the rich aroma filled the air, offering a brief comfort. The clock on the wall ticked

softly, its hands creeping toward 3 AM. I poured the steaming liquid into a travel mug, my mind

buzzing with thoughts of the upcoming race.

"Early bird or night owl?" Melody's voice cut through the stillness, laced with laughter. She came into the kitchen bright-eyed and cheerful—a stark contrast to the exhaustion I felt clinging to my bones.

"Definitely an early bird," I replied, forcing a smile as I turned to face her. "Got a lot on my mind."

She leaned against the counter, crossing her arms with a playful smirk. "Are you sure it's not just the pressure of the big race? I mean, we all know you're a workaholic, but you've really taken it to the next level."

I chuckled softly, knowing she was right. "You could say that. Just trying to make sure everything runs smoothly. Phantom's counting on me."

"Uh-huh," she said, feigning disbelief. "And what about you? You can't pour from an empty cup, Steph. You need to take care of yourself too. The ranch needs you to be healthy and strong, and I can't have my best friend turning into a caffeine-fueled zombie."

Her playful concern brought a warmth to my chest, and I couldn't help but roll my eyes at her antics. "I'm fine, Melody. Just a little caffeine to kickstart the day. I promise I'll get some sleep after the race."

"After the race? Please," she scoffed, waving a hand dismissively. "You'll probably be so hyped up on adrenaline that you'll want to celebrate all night. Just promise me you won't forget to eat, okay?

I'm not about to let you starve yourself in the name of ranching."

I laughed, the tension easing a bit in my shoulders. "I promise I'll eat. I'll even make a point to sit down and enjoy a meal—maybe even one you cook."

"Now we're talking," she grinned, grabbing a muffin from the counter and tossing it my way. "Here, take this for the road. It's not a full breakfast, but it's better than nothing."

"Thanks," I said, catching the muffin and popping it into my bag. "I really appreciate your looking out for me."

"Always," Melody replied, her tone softening. "But seriously, you need to let loose a little. I mean, it's not just about the race. There's more to life than work, you know?"

Her words hung in the air and I felt a pang of reality wash over me. The weight of the upcoming race, the fear of losing the ranch, and the unspoken tension between Ashlyn and me had become all-consuming. It was easy to lose sight of everything else. "I know, I just . . . I feel like there's so much at stake right now," I confessed, my voice barely above a whisper. "If Phantom doesn't win, we could lose everything. And I can't let that happen."

Melody stepped closer, placing a reassuring hand on my shoulder. "You've worked hard to get to this point, Steph. Just remember that you're not in this alone. You've got me, and you've got Ashlyn. Lean on us a little, okay?"

Her words resonated deep within me and I nodded, grateful for Melody's unwavering support. Did I have Ashlyn, though? I wanted to believe in our connection, so very much. But, something wasn't right between us. "You're right. I just need to keep my focus on the race for now. Once it's over, I'll take a breather."

"Good plan," she said, eyes sparkling with mischief. "And maybe after you win, we can have a celebratory bonfire. Get some s'mores going and reminisce about how you single-handedly saved the ranch with your mad skills and Ashlyn's incredible riding."

"Deal," I replied, my spirits lifting at the

thought of a celebration. "But only if you promise to make those fancy hot dogs you love."

"Only if you promise to actually eat one this time!" Melody shot back, her laughter filling the kitchen as I grabbed my things and headed for the door.

"Okay, I'm in. See you later!" I called over my shoulder, the warmth of our banter lingering as I stepped out into the crisp morning air. I settled into my truck, ready to face another day of preparations for the race. I just couldn't shake the feeling that this was more than "just a race." It was a turning point for all of us, and I was determined to rise to the occasion—no matter what it took.

~

The soft glow of the moon filtered through the curtains, casting gentle shadows across the room as I lay nestled beside Ashlyn. The world outside was wrapped in quiet stillness, a stark contrast to

the whirlwind of thoughts that had led up to this moment. Tonight, all the tension and doubts that had clouded my mind melted away, leaving only the warmth of her presence beside me.

I turned my head to watch her as she slept, her

features softened in the moonlight. Her hair spilled across the pillow like liquid gold, and I couldn't keep myself from reaching out to tuck a stray lock behind her ear. Ashlyn stirred slightly, a faint smile gracing her lips even in her sleep, and my heart swelled at the sight.

This race was the culmination of so much hard work and dedication—both for Phantom and for us. It loomed large on the horizon, a challenge that could change everything. Yet here in this moment, it felt like nothing else mattered. All the noise and chaos of the world faded away, leaving just the two of us cocooned in our own little haven. As I shifted closer, I felt the warmth radiating from her body. It was comforting, grounding me in a way that I desperately needed. I wrapped my arms around Ashlyn, pulling her close. Savoring the feel of her against me. Ashlyn's body fit perfectly against mine, and I relished the intimacy of this quiet moment. We had a connection that transcended words—a silent understanding of everything we had been through together.

"Hey," I whispered, my voice barely breaking the silence. She stirred again, her lids fluttering open to reveal those captivating eyes that seemed to hold galaxies within them.

"Hey," she murmured, a sleepy smile blooming on her face as she took in the sight of me. "What time is it?"

"Too late for you to be worried about the race," I replied playfully, brushing my fingers along her arm. "We've done everything we can. Tomorrow, we just need to trust ourselves and Phantom."

"Right," she said, her voice still thick with sleep. "I just can't help but feel a little anxious."

I nodded, understanding her perfectly. I felt it too—the tight knot of nerves in my stomach and the uncertainty of what lay ahead. But as I held her close, I realized that this moment was ours. No matter the outcome, we would still have each other. "Whatever happens tomorrow, I want you to know how proud I am of you. You've poured your heart into Phantom and he's lucky to have you."

A soft blush crept across her cheeks and I felt a flutter of joy at the sight. "You really think so?" she asked, her voice barely above a whisper.

"I know so," I replied earnestly. "You've been incredible. I believe in you, Ashlyn."

She shifted slightly, propping herself up on one elbow to meet my gaze. "You always know how to make me feel better," she said, her tone turning serious. "But it's more than that. You've been my rock through all of this."

I smiled, brushing my fingers along her jawline, reveling in the closeness. "We're a team, remember? I'm here for you, just like you're here for me." A moment of silence passed between us, charged with unspoken feelings. I could see the way her expression shifted, a mixture of vulnerability and something deeper simmering just beneath the surface. And then, without thinking, I leaned in closer, capturing her lips with mine in a soft kiss that spoke volumes about the connection we shared.

As we pulled apart, I felt the need to express everything that had been building inside me. "Ashlyn," I began, my heart pounding in my chest. "I love you."

Her eyes widened, a mixture of surprise and delight flooding her features. "You love me?" she echoed, as if savoring the words.

"Yeah," I said, my voice steady despite the rush of emotions. "I do. I've loved you for a while now. It's just—everything feels so uncertain right now, but I know that my feelings for you are real.

You've brought so much joy into my life."

The corners of her mouth turned up into a

radiant smile and I felt my heart soar. "I love you too, Stephanie," she said, her voice warm and genuine. "I've been scared to say it, but I feel it in every moment we spend together."

We fell into another kiss, this one deeper and more passionate, igniting a fire between us that chased away the shadows of uncertainty. As we held each other close, I knew that no matter what

tomorrow brought, we would face it together. The love we shared was a force that could weather any storm, and that thought filled me with an unwavering strength.

As we lay together, our bodies entwined under the soft sheets, I allowed myself to drift into a peaceful sleep, comforted by the knowledge that we had each other, no matter what the future

held. The race, the challenges, and all the doubts would come and go, but this bond we had created was something I cherished above all else. And for now, that was enough.

20

ASHLYN

I could only describe my morning, my thoughts, and my mind as a series of snapshots. The alarm blared, pulling me from a dream filled with galloping horses and the smell of fresh hay. I blinked against the morning light streaming through the window, my heart pounding with a mix of excitement and anxiety. Today was the day. I swung my legs over the edge of the bed, my feet hitting the cool floor, and took a moment to gather my thoughts. Phantom's big moment was finally here.

In the kitchen, I poured a cup of coffee, the rich aroma filling the air and giving me a much-needed boost. I could hear the faint sounds of

Stephanie and Melody moving around in the background,

their laughter and chatter a comforting reminder of the support around me. I took a deep breath, trying to ground myself, visualizing Phantom and me crossing the finish line strong and victorious.

As the sun began to rise higher in the sky, I slipped into my riding boots and grabbed Phantom's gear. The barn was alive with activity, the sound of hooves on the ground echoing in the air. I approached Phantom in his stall and he nickered softly at me, his big brown eyes sparkling with energy. "Ready for today, big guy?" I murmured, giving him a gentle pat on the neck. We were a team, and I could feel the connection between us. I led him out and began loading him into the horse trailer, my heart racing as I secured him for the ride.

The drive to the venue was a blur of landscapes flashing past—fields of wildflowers, clusters of trees, and the occasional glimpse of fellow competitors on the road. My heart raced with each mile we covered, anticipation building within me. "Just stay calm," I whispered to Phantom, who shifted nervously in the trailer. I could feel the adrenaline surging through my veins. The excitement mingling with the inevitable nerves that accompanied any big race.

As we pulled into the venue, the atmosphere hit me like a wave. The place was bustling with activity, a hive of energy and noise. Horses whinnied in the distance and the air was filled with the scent of hay, leather, and a hint of sweat. My stomach fluttered with a mix of excitement and anxiety as I stepped out of the truck. I took a moment to absorb it all—the tents, the crowd, and the other riders preparing their horses. This was it.

With quick movements, I unloaded Phantom and led him to the warm-up area. People were everywhere—trainers shouting instructions, spectators milling about, and the buzz of conversations

creating an atmosphere of excitement. I felt the weight of the crowd's expectations but I pushed it aside, focusing on Phantom. I brushed him down, the rhythmic motion calming both him and me. "Let's

show them what we can do," I said softly, looking into his eyes. He responded with a gentle nicker.

Once Phantom was saddled and ready, I took a moment to adjust my gear, feeling the familiar light weight of the saddle beneath my hands. I had made sure to lose a few pounds to make sure I was lean enough to race and I felt ready. My heart raced in my chest, each beat echoing the pulse of the crowd outside. I tightened the straps, ensuring everything was secure, and stepped back to admire my horse. He was magnificent, a picture of power and grace. "You're going to shine today," I promised him, giving him a gentle pat before slipping on my helmet covered in Stephanie's sky blue silks.

As we made our way to the starting line, energy surged through me like electricity. The cheers from the crowd filled the air and I could see other competitors lining up, their horses pawing at the ground. Mirroring my own anticipation. Adrenaline pumped through my veins, sharpening my focus. The world around me faded as I concentrated on the task ahead. It was Phantom and me against the rest.

We took our place at the starting gates. I could hear my heart pounding in my ears, each beat syncing with the rhythm of the moment. I adjusted my grip on the reins, feeling the horse's power beneath me, and glanced sideways at the other riders. Their eyes were fixed forward, but I was solely focused on Phantom. "Let's do this, buddy," I whispered, leaning forward in the saddle as the countdown began.

The gates opened and we burst forward, surging forward from the starting line, the adrenaline coursing through my veins like wildfire. Phantom felt powerful beneath me, his muscles coiling and uncoiling. The world around us became a blur—spectators cheering, the sound of hoofbeats pounding against the earth, and the intoxicating rush of wind filling my lungs.

But I could feel tension in Phantom's body. He was eager, but I sensed he hadn't quite found his rhythm. As we rounded the first turn, I leaned forward, urging him on. The other horses jostled for position, their riders shouting commands, but Phantom remained steady. I squeezed my legs against his sides, encouraging him to pick up the pace, yet he was still holding back—seemingly unsure of the

chaos around him. The first few minutes felt like an eternity. I could feel my heart sinking as we began to lag behind the pack.

The second turn came and I could see the leading horses pulling ahead. My breath quickened as I fought against the knot of anxiety tightening in my chest. "Come on, Phantom!" I urged him, my

voice barely rising above the noise of the crowd. "We've trained for this! Let's go!"

It wasn't until we hit the third turn that Phantom's true power erupted. Something shifted within him, a spark igniting as he found his stride. Suddenly, he surged forward, his hooves pounding against

the dirt as if he had been holding back all along. I felt a rush of exhilaration as he kicked into a high gear, his muscles flexing and straining with every powerful stride. "That's it! That's it!" I shouted, my voice full of encouragement. With each passing second, we gained ground, darting past horses that had previously been ahead

of us. I could feel the sheer force of his speed, the way he powered through the bend, and I was in awe of how seamlessly we moved as one. The world around us faded into a blur of colors, the cheers of the crowd transforming into a distant roar. Phantom was flying now, and it felt like we were defying gravity.

As we approached the final stretch, the crowd erupted into a deafening cheer, their excitement palpable. I focused ahead, zeroing in on the leading horse, a grey, who was just a few lengths

ahead. My heart raced as I realized we had a chance. I leaned forward, gripping the reins with determination, and whispered, "Let's do this!"

Phantom responded, his stride lengthening as he pushed himself even harder. The finishing line drew closer, the tension in the air electrifying. With every ounce of energy he had left, Phantom thundered toward the finish line. I could feel the sweat on his neck and the determination radiating from his body as he charged ahead. We were neck-and-neck with the grey, and I could see the finish line approaching like a beacon of hope.

But as we crossed the line, I felt a bittersweet ache in my chest. We had given everything, and though we didn't take first place, we had stormed in a close second. I should have got him to raise his gear sooner. I should have done better. I knew Phantom was the fastest horse out there, but I had not been the best for him. Phantom's hooves pounded to a halt and I quickly dismounted, barely able to contain the tears that welled in my eyes. I wrapped my arms around his neck, breathing in the scent of sweat and hay, overwhelmed by a surge of joy and pride.

"You were incredible!" I cried, my voice cracking with emotion. The announcer's voice echoed over the loudspeakers, confirming our second-place finish and a prize of $50,000. I could hardly believe it! It wasn't first, but it was certainly something.

It would give us more time to do more and he had been magnificent. I felt pride burst from me. Tears streamed down my face, a mix of relief and joy washing over me. We had done it. Phantom had proven

himself. The ranch was safe. And in that moment, nothing else mattered.

Surrounded by the chaos of celebrating spectators, I buried my face in Phantom's mane, overwhelmed by the sheer thrill of our performance. We hadn't won, but we had shown the world what we were capable of, which felt like victory enough.

21

STEPHANIE

They had crossed the finish line in a blur and I could see the numbers flashing— second place.

It wasn't the victory we had hoped for, but it was still a remarkable achievement. I felt tears prick at the corners of my eyes as I took in the scene. They had given it everything they had and Ashlyn was on her knees, tears of joy streaming down her face as she embraced Phantom.

I rushed forward, my heart swelling with pride and relief. "You did it, Ashlyn! You were amazing!" I cried, wrapping my arms around her and Phantom. As she buried her face in Phantom's mane, I felt a rush of gratitude wash over me. They had brought us back from the brink. Even though we didn't take first place, the $50,000 prize would make a world of difference. We could save the ranch. In that moment, as I held Ashlyn close, I realized how deeply I loved her and how much she meant to me.

Despite the challenges we faced, I knew we were stronger together. Ashlyn had fought through her fears and I had watched her transform into the incredible rider I always knew she could be. And as we stood there, surrounded by the chaos of celebration, I couldn't help but feel that this was just the beginning of something extraordinary.

I pulled Ashlyn close, feeling the warmth radiating from her body as we kissed, our hearts soaring with the thrill of the race. The world around us faded and for a moment, it was just the two of us, basking in the joy of our hard-fought success. I could feel the weight of the past few weeks lift off my shoulders. All that mattered now was the love I felt for her.

But then I felt Ashlyn stiffen in my arms, her body tensing as if a chill had swept through the air. I pulled back slightly, searching her face for the source of her sudden change. That's when I noticed the woman approaching us, her expression a mix of smugness and disdain.

"Good race, Ashlyn," she sneered, her tone dripping with sarcasm. I could sense the ice in the air, and how Ashlyn's mood had shifted from elation to something darker. The warmth we had just shared

felt like a distant memory as tension crackled between us.

"Thanks," Ashlyn replied coolly, her voice barely above a whisper, her gaze locked onto the woman as if she were sizing her up. I could see the flicker of defiance in her eyes, but there was also an undercurrent of fear there that made my heart ache for her.

"What are you doing here?" Ashlyn's words were sharp, cutting through the celebratory atmosphere like a knife. I felt a surge of protectiveness wash over me, wanting to shield Ashlyn from whatever this woman represented.

"Oh, I just came to congratulate you on your little win," the woman replied, her smirk widening. "Well, second place, wasn't it?"

The words hung in the air like heavy fog, and I could see Ashlyn's expression harden.

22

ASHLYN

I stood there, still reeling from the emotions of the race. Celebrating the incredible run that Phantom and I had just completed.

Then the joy and pride that had filled my heart began to wither away, replaced by an icy dread as Monica approached. She moved through the crowd with a grace that belied the malice in her eyes, her presence commanding attention like a dark storm cloud descending over a sunny day.

Monica was devastatingly beautiful, as always. Her hair perfectly styled, her outfit impeccable, and her smile a razor-sharp weapon hidden behind a veil of sophistication. The time we had spent apart hadn't dulled her allure. If anything, it had only sharpened the edges of her charm. But I knew better than anyone the poison that lurked beneath that polished exterior.

As she closed the distance between us, I felt my body go rigid, the warmth of Stephanie's embrace slipping away as the cold reality of Monica's arrival settled in. My heart pounded in my chest, not with the adrenaline of victory, but with a growing sense of dread.

"Good race, Ashlyn," Monica sneered, her voice laced with a venomous sweetness. The words dripped with sarcasm—a deliberate mockery of everything I had just accomplished. My hands, which had been holding Stephanie so tenderly just moments ago, clenched into fists at my sides as I fought to maintain my composure.

Stephanie's arms loosened around me as she sensed the shift, her gaze flicking between Monica and me, confusion and concern etched on her face. I could see the questions forming in her mind, but before she could ask, Monica turned her attention to her, a predatory smile curling on her lips.

"And you must be Stephanie Morley," Monica purred, her tone dripping with faux politeness.

"I've heard so much about you. Tell me, how does it feel to be the latest in a long line of owners to catch Ashlyn's eye? She has a kink for an older woman who is employing her, but then, I'm sure you know that."

The words hung in the air like a slap, the insult barely veiled. I saw Stephanie's eyes widen in shock, her brows knitting together as she processed the barb. My stomach churned with guilt and anger—anger at Monica for her cruelty and guilt for the secrets I had kept from Stephanie.

Monica didn't stop there, however. She stepped closer to Stephanie, her gaze cutting like a knife. "Did you know, darling, that Ashlyn can never race again in Kentucky? Funny, isn't it? As talented as she is, banned from the entire state. But then again, that's what happens when you choose sex and money over everything."

I felt as if the ground had been ripped out from under me. The truth, which I had kept hidden so carefully, was now laid bare in the most brutal way possible. Stephanie's face paled and I saw the hurt flash in her eyes as the weight of Monica's words sank in.

"Monica, stop," I hissed, stepping forward, my voice trembling with a mix of desperation and fury. "This isn't about you. This has nothing to do with you."

But Monica just laughed—a cold, hollow sound that sent shivers down my spine. "Oh, but it has everything to do with me, Ashlyn. You think you can just walk away from what we had, from what I gave you, and start fresh? You think you can hide who you really are?"

Her words cut deep, each one like a knife twisting in my gut. I could feel Stephanie's gaze burning into me, her silence louder than any accusation she could have made. I had wanted to protect her from this, from the ugliness of my past, but now it was too late.

"I never hid anything from you," I shot back, my voice shaking with emotion. "What we had ... it was a mistake, and I've paid for it every day since."

Monica's eyes narrowed, the mask of charm slipping to reveal the bitterness beneath. "A mistake?

Is that what you call it? You used me, Ashlyn. You took everything I gave you, and then you walked away when you got what you wanted. But you can't run from your past forever."

I felt a lump forming in my throat as I turned

to Stephanie, my heart breaking at the hurt and confusion in her eyes. "Stephanie, I . . . I didn't want you to find out like this. I was going to tell you, I swear. But it's not what she's making it out to be."

Stephanie stared at me, her expression unreadable, and I could feel the distance growing between us with every passing second. The connection we had shared, the love that had blossomed between us, now felt fragile, like it was on the verge of shattering under the weight of the truth.

Monica's smile widened as she saw the impact of her words, satisfied with the chaos she had sown. "Good luck with your *little* texan ranch, Ashlyn. I wonder how long it will take before you get bored and move on to the next owner with short skirts and deep pockets."

With that, she turned on her heel and walked away, leaving a trail of devastation in her wake. I stood there, frozen, as the world around me seemed to crumble. Stephanie remained silent, her eyes fixed on the ground, and I could feel the wall between us growing taller, thicker, and surely impossible to breach.

"Stephanie," I whispered, my voice choked with emotion. "Please, just let me explain."

She looked up at me, her eyes filled with a mix of hurt, betrayal, and something else—something that looked dangerously close to resignation. "Explain what, Ashlyn? That you've been lying to

me? That there's this whole part of your life I knew nothing about?"

"I didn't want to lie to you," I pleaded, stepping closer, but she took a step back, the distance between us growing. "I just . . . I didn't want to lose you. I didn't want my past to ruin what we have."

She shook her head, her expression hardening. "You should have trusted me. You should have told me the truth."

Her words hit me like a punch to the gut and I felt the tears welling up in my eyes. "I'm sorry, Stephanie. I'm so sorry. I didn't know how to tell you. I didn't want to hurt you."

She looked at me for a long moment, her gaze searching mine, and I could see the conflict in her eyes. But then she shook her head again, her shoulders slumping with a sadness that tore at my heart. "I need some time, Ashlyn. I need to think."

With that, she turned and walked away, leaving

me standing there, alone in the midst of the crowd, my heart breaking as I watched her go. The joy of the race, the love we had shared, now felt like a distant memory that had been overshadowed by the darkness of my past. And it had finally caught up with me.

23

STEPHANIE

Days passed like a blur, each one melding into the next, marked only by the routines of the ranch and the hollow emptiness that had settled in my chest. The vibrant energy that had once filled my life—the excitement of the race, the thrill of being with Ashlyn, all of it—had been replaced by a cold, hard resolve. I wouldn't allow myself to be a victim again. I wouldn't let anyone else close enough to hurt me.

The morning after that disastrous encounter with Monica, I woke to an empty bed, the absence of Ashlyn's warmth beside me a stark reminder of the growing distance between us. I had thought that maybe, just maybe, love could be different this time. That perhaps, in Ashlyn, I had found someone who could see past the scars, both physical and emotional, that life had left on me.

But I had been wrong. Humans were predators by nature and I had been foolish to think otherwise. I threw myself into work on the ranch with a ferocity that left little room for anything else. The

rhythm of the days became my anchor. The tasks of caring for the horses, managing the land, and overseeing the finances filled every waking moment. I didn't have time to think about Ashlyn, nor about the way she had shattered the fragile trust I'd placed in her. The ranch was my life now, and my only focus.

Days turned into weeks and the memory of Ashlyn's touch, her smile, and the way she looked at me like I was something precious—all that began to fade. It was better this way, I told myself. Better to bury those memories deep, where they couldn't hurt me anymore.

I stopped answering her calls and deleted her texts without even reading them. Every time my phone buzzed, my heart would leap with a cruel hope, only to be crushed again as I forced myself to ignore it. I couldn't let Ashlyn back in. I wouldn't give her the chance to lie to me again.

Melody noticed, of course. She tried to talk to me, tried to get me to open up, but I shut her down every time. "I'm fine," I would say, my voice clipped, leaving no room for argument. "Just busy with the ranch."

But she knew better. She could see the change in me, the way I had closed myself off, retreating behind the walls I had spent years building. The walls that had crumbled when Ashlyn walked into my life, only to be rebuilt stronger, higher than ever before.

The nights were the hardest. Alone in the big, empty house, I would lie awake, staring at the ceiling, replaying every moment I had spent with Ashlyn. I would hear her laughter in the silence, feel the ghost of her touch against my skin. But those memories, once a source of comfort, had turned into daggers, each one cutting deeper than the last.

I buried those thoughts as best I could and tried to focus on the tangible things—the horses, the land, and the numbers that needed balancing. The ranch was thriving, at least. Phantom's performance at the race had brought in enough money to keep us secure for a while, and I had Bill's support in managing the finances.

But even that victory felt hollow, tainted by the knowledge of how it had come to be.

More weeks passed and the days grew shorter as summer bled into autumn. The mornings were crisp, the air carrying the scent of earth and fallen leaves. I found solace in the early hours, watching the sun rise over the hills. The world was so quiet and still before the day's work began.

But even during those peaceful moments, there was an ache in my chest, a hollow place that refused to be filled. The few times I ventured into town, I caught glimpses of couples walking hand in hand, their laughter floating on the breeze, and it would twist something deep inside me. I had tried to believe in love again, but love had proven to be as cruel and deceptive as I had always feared.

One day, as I was fixing the fence along the northern pasture, Melody approached me, her face etched with concern. "Stephanie," she began hesitantly, "you can't keep doing this. You can't keep

shutting everyone out."

"I'm not shutting anyone out," I snapped, the

words harsher than I intended. "I'm just focused on the ranch."

"Don't lie to me," she said softly, her eyes searching mine. "You're hurting and I can see it. But pushing people away isn't going to make the pain go away."

I turned away from her, focusing on the task at hand, refusing to let her words break through the armor I had built around myself. "I'm fine, Melody. Just let it go."

She sighed, a sound filled with frustration and sadness. "I just don't want you to lose yourself in this. You deserve better."

Better. The word echoed in my mind long after Melody walked away, but it held no meaning for me anymore. "Better" was an illusion, a lie I had told myself when I had let Ashlyn into my heart. The reality was that people were selfish and deceitful—and ultimately, out for themselves. Love was just a weapon, one that left deep, festering wounds.

So I worked day after day, pouring every ounce of energy into the ranch, into the horses, and into the land that had become my sanctuary. And slowly, the pain began to dull, replaced by a cold numbness that I welcomed with open arms.

Ashlyn had been removed from my life, and I wouldn't let anyone else in. Not again. Not ever. The ranch was all that mattered now, and I would protect it—and protect myself—at any cost.

24

MELODY

As I stepped onto the familiar path leading to the barn, the gentle sound of hooves on gravel echoed in my ears, a soothing reminder of the life I had built alongside Stephanie. The sun illuminated the vibrant hues of the wildflowers that had stubbornly pushed their way through the cracked earth.

This place had become my sanctuary, a refuge from the chaos of my past. I had come to the ranch seeking shelter from a storm. In the process, I had found not only safety, but a family in Stephanie.

In the beginning, I had kept my distance, reluctant to share the scars of my history. But Stephanie had a way of making me feel at home without pressing for answers. She respected my silence, never prying too deep. Allowing me to reveal my truths at my own pace. It was one of her greatest qualities—the ability to nurture without suffocating, to support without demanding. As a result, I blossomed like the wildflowers around me, gradually shedding the weight of my past and learning to embrace the present.

But as the weeks turned into months, I couldn't help but notice the shadow that had settled over Stephanie. She was usually a beacon of light, radiating warmth and positivity, but now her laughter was less frequent and her eyes held a depth of sorrow that I couldn't ignore. There was an emptiness in her gaze, a silence that spoke louder than words. I could sense that something was off, and that the walls she had built around her heart were slowly closing in.

I worried for her, and after a while, a sense of urgency washed over me. I needed to help Stephanie, to break through the invisible barrier that had formed between us. It was hard to watch someone so vibrant become a shell of her former self, and I was determined to do whatever it took to bring her back to life.

"Hey, Steph!" I called out as I entered the barn, spotting her leaning against the stall door, deep in thought. The soft whicker of the horses welcomed me as I approached, and I felt a flutter of hope that perhaps today would be different.

She turned at the sound of my voice, her lips curling into a faint smile that didn't quite reach her eyes. "Hey, Melody. Just . . . thinking," she replied, her voice carrying a weight I hadn't heard before.

I took a step closer, concern etched across my face. "Is everything okay? You've seemed a bit . . . off lately. You know I'm here if you want to talk, right?"

She hesitated, the flicker of vulnerability passing through her features before she masked it with a shrug. "Yeah, I know. Just . . . a lot on my mind, I guess." Her words were a gentle reminder of her

usual reluctance to share. I felt a pang of frustration mixed with empathy.

"Stephanie, you don't have to carry the world on your shoulders alone. Whatever it is, I'm here. You don't have to pretend to be strong for me." I stepped closer, hoping to bridge the distance between us.

For a moment her facade cracked, and I caught a glimpse of the turmoil swirling beneath the surface. "It's just . . . everything with Ashlyn. It's complicated," she finally admitted, her voice barely

above a whisper.

The mention of Ashlyn sent a rush of understanding through me. I had witnessed the bond they shared, and how the love that was supposed to be a lifeline had somehow turned into a source of pain.

"What happened? You can talk to me," I urged gently, my heart aching for her.

Stephanie sighed, running a hand through her hair in a gesture of frustration. "I don't know, Mel. I thought everything was perfect, but now it feels like it's all falling apart." Her voice trembled slightly. "I've always believed in love, but now I'm starting to see it differently. Humans are predators, Mel. They take what they want and leave behind a mess for someone else to clean up."

I reached for her hand, squeezing it tightly as I met her gaze. "You're not a victim, Stephanie.

You've fought so hard to build this place, to create something beautiful. Just like I have. We can't let others define who we are or what we believe in."

She nodded slowly, her eyes glistening with unshed tears. "I want to believe that, but it's hard when someone you care about hurts you. Lies to you."

"Maybe it's time to confront her," I suggested gently. "Sometimes the hardest conversations lead to the most important truths. You deserve clarity and so does Ashlyn."

Stephanie remained quiet, her mind clearly racing with thoughts. The weight of her worries was palpable and I knew I had to stand by her side, to remind Stephanie of the strength that resided within her.

"I'm with you, no matter what. Just remember that," I added, squeezing her hand one more time before releasing it.

As I watched her gaze drift back toward the horses, I silently vowed to support Stephanie through whatever lay ahead. She had pulled me from the shadows of my past and now it was my turn to help her find her way back to the light. The ranch was our sanctuary. Together, we would weather whatever storm came our way, one step at a time.

I arrived at the small café early, choosing a table by the window where I could keep an eye on the street. My heart was heavy with the weight of the conversation I knew was coming. I had seen Stephanie's pain, the way she had withdrawn into herself after Ashlyn had left. I hated seeing her like that—so closed off, so distant from the person I knew.

And now, sitting here, waiting for Ashlyn, I felt a mix of emotions. Part of me wanted to protect Stephanie, to shield her from more hurt, but another part of me believed that everyone deserves a chance to tell their story.

When Ashlyn walked through the door, I almost didn't recognize her. The striking beauty that had once captivated so many was still there, but it was hidden beneath layers of hurt, tiredness, and

something that looked like deep-seated loneliness. Her face was pale and drawn below her cowboy hat. Her hair looked like shit. She carried herself with a weight I hadn't seen before. As she approached the table, I could see the desperation in her eyes.

"Melody," she said softly, her voice tinged with

exhaustion as she slid into the seat across from me. "Thank you for meeting me."

I nodded, taking in her appearance. Her hair, usually so perfectly styled, hung limply around her face. Dark circles shadowed her eyes and there was a hollowness to her cheeks that spoke of sleepless nights and endless worry. This wasn't the Ashlyn I had first met—the confident, vibrant, almost intimidating woman who had won Stephanie's heart.

This was someone broken, someone who had lost her way.

"Of course," I replied, my tone careful and measured. "But let's be clear from the start, Ashlyn. I'm not here to plead your case to Stephanie."

Her eyes widened and I saw the flicker of hope in them dim slightly. "I—" she began, but I held up a hand, stopping her.

"I mean it," I said firmly. "This isn't about me convincing Stephanie to give you another chance. She's been through a lot, and I won't do anything that could hurt her more than she already has been."

Ashlyn looked down at her hands, which were trembling slightly. For a moment, she didn't say anything. I could see her trying to compose herself. When she finally looked up at me, her eyes were filled with a raw, desperate need.

"I know I messed up," she said, her voice barely above a whisper. "I know I hurt her, and it kills me to think that I might have lost her for good. But Melody, please—if I could just talk to her, explain everything..."

There it was, the pleading I had been expecting. I could see the regret etched into every line of her face, but I couldn't let myself be swayed by it. Stephanie was my priority, and I needed to be sure that this was the right thing to do.

"Ashlyn," I said, my voice softening just a fraction, "I'm not going to make any promises. But I do believe that everyone deserves a chance to tell their side of the story. If you're willing to be honest with her, to really lay it all out there, I'll arrange for you to come to the ranch and talk to Stephanie. But you have to promise me something."

She nodded quickly, relief washing over her features. "Anything," she said, the desperation in her voice unmistakable.

"I need you to promise that you'll be honest. No more secrets, no more half-truths. Stephanie deserves to know everything, and she deserves to hear it from you. And more than that, I need you to promise that you'll be the woman I know you can be. Not just for her, but for yourself. You have to be better than the person who hurt her."

Ashlyn swallowed hard, her eyes glistening with unshed tears. "I promise, Melody," she said, her voice trembling. "I'll be honest with her, and I'll do whatever it takes to make things right."

I studied her for a long moment, searching her face for any sign of deceit. But all I saw was sincerity and a deep regret that seemed to emanate from her very soul. I wanted to believe her. I wanted to believe that people could change. That Ashlyn could be the woman Stephanie needed her to be.

"Okay," I finally said, leaning back in my chair. "I'll talk to Stephanie. But remember, Ashlyn, this is your chance to make things right. Don't waste it."

Ashlyn nodded, her expression a mixture of hope and determination. "Thank you, Melody. I won't waste it. I promise."

As I watched her leave the café, shoulders slumped under the weight of the world that she carried, I couldn't help but feel a pang of empathy for her. Ashlyn was fighting her own demons, just as

Stephanie was, and maybe—just maybe—this conversation could lead to something good.

But as I walked back to the ranch, I knew that the road ahead was uncertain. Stephanie had built walls around her heart, and breaking through them wouldn't be easy. But if there was one thing I had learned from my own journey, it was that sometimes, you had to face the darkness before you could find the light.

25

STEPHANIE

The sun cast long shadows across the rolling hills as I rode Phantom through the familiar trails of the ranch. The rhythmic thud of his hooves against the earth matched the steady beat of my heart, a comforting rhythm that usually brought me solace. But today, as I

guided him through the winding paths, I could feel a heaviness in the air—a sadness that seemed to seep from his very soul.

Phantom had always been a powerful horse, strong and spirited, yet today he felt different. There was a yearning in his movements, a longing that echoed the unspoken tension that had settled over the ranch since Ashlyn's departure. I could sense his unease, his restlessness, and it mirrored my own tumultuous emotions.

"Come on, buddy," I murmured, urging him forward, but the gentle pressure of my legs against his sides seemed to only deepen his melancholy. It was as if he were aware of the absence of the one person who had truly understood him, the one who had taught him calm amongst the chaos. I could almost hear the whispers of his heart. He missed Ashlyn as much as I did.

As we neared the stables, Phantom's ears perked up and I felt a surge of excitement pulse through him. He began to whinny, a sound filled with both hope and anticipation. I could sense the shift in his demeanor. He was eager to see Ashlyn again, to feel her presence near him once more.

"Easy, boy," I said softly, patting his neck as I dismounted. I couldn't help but smile at his enthusiasm, even if it tugged at my own heartstrings. The bond we shared was unbreakable, built on trust and respect. But now, it felt strained under the weight of unspoken words and unresolved feelings.

As I entered the stables, the familiar scent enveloped me, bringing with it a sense of comfort. But that comfort was short-lived when I caught sight of Ashlyn standing there, her cowgirl silhouette framed by the fading light. She was brushing down one of the other horses, her movements fluid and practiced, yet there was an air of vulnerability about her that struck me.

The moment our eyes met, I felt the air between us crackle with an intensity that made my heart race. Ashlyn's gaze was filled with a mixture of longing and uncertainty. I couldn't help but feel

a pang of empathy for her. She looked so beautiful, even with the shadows lingering beneath her eyes. A testament to the sleepless nights and restless thoughts that had clearly haunted her as they had me since she left.

Phantom stepped forward, his excitement palpable, and I could see how Ashlyn's expression brightened at the sight of him. It was as if a light had flickered back to life in her eyes. I watched in silence as she approached, her hands reaching out to stroke his powerful neck. The

connection between them was undeniable. An unspoken bond that transcended words.

Seeing her there, so close yet so distant, brought a flood of emotions rushing to the surface. I was happy to see her, yes, but that happiness was tangled up in a web of hurt and betrayal that I hadn't fully processed. The way she had left, the secrets she had kept—it had all left a deep wound that hadn't yet healed. And now, standing in front of her, those old wounds felt fresh, as if no time had passed at all.

I watched as she interacted with Phantom, the tenderness in her touch and the way she seemed to find solace in his presence. It reminded me of the connection we had once shared, a connection that now felt like it was teetering on the edge of a precipice. Part of me wanted to reach out, to bridge the gap between us, but another part held back, guarded, unwilling to let go of the pain that still lingered.

Ashlyn looked up at me, her eyes searching mine, as if trying to gauge my reaction. I held her gaze for a moment, feeling the unspoken words hanging heavy in the air between us. There was so much to say, so much that needed to be addressed. But I wasn't ready. Not yet.

Without a word, I turned away, focusing on unfastening Phantom's bridle and leading him into his stall. My movements were mechanical, methodical, a way to keep my emotions in check. I could feel Ashlyn's presence behind me, the weight of her gaze like a physical touch. But I didn't turn around.

As I tended to Phantom, brushing down his coat and murmuring soothing words to him, I tried to steady my breathing, to calm the storm of emotions that threatened to overwhelm me. I wasn't sure

how to feel. Wasn't sure if I could ever truly forgive her for the way she had left, and for the secrets she had kept.

When I finally turned back, Ashlyn was still standing there, her eyes filled with a mixture of hope and apprehension. I wanted to say something, anything, but the words caught in my throat.

Instead, I simply nodded at her, a small gesture that I hoped conveyed the complex emotions I couldn't yet articulate.

Without another word, I walked past her, feeling the tension between us like a taut wire ready to snap. As I left the stables, the cool evening air hit my face, and I let out a breath I hadn't realized I had been holding.

I stepped out of the stables and the cool evening air wrapped around me, offering a brief respite from the storm of emotions that churned inside me. I was just about to head back to the house when I heard footsteps behind me, quick and urgent. I didn't need to turn around to know who it was—Ashlyn.

"Stephanie, wait!" Her voice was breathless, desperate, and before I could react, she was in front of me, blocking my path. Her eyes were wide, pleading, and I could see the strain in every line of her face. "Please, just listen to me."

I felt a tightness in my chest, a wave of conflicting emotions crashing over me. I wanted to walk away, to shield myself from whatever she was about to say, but something in her voice, in the raw vulnerability etched on her face, made me pause.

"Ashlyn . . . " I began, but she cut me off, her voice trembling.

"Please, Stephanie. I know I messed up. I know I hurt you, and I can't even begin to express how sorry I am. But I need you to give me one more chance. Just one more chance to explain, to tell you everything." Her words tumbled out in a rush, as if she was afraid that if she stopped speaking, I would slip away.

I looked at her, really looked at her, and I could see the weight of her regret, the desperation in her eyes. It was clear that whatever she had been holding back had taken its toll on her, and that she was laying it all out in front of me now, raw and exposed.

"Ashlyn, I . . ." I tried again, my voice faltering. The walls I had built around my heart felt like they were crumbling, but the hurt was still there, too fresh, too deep. "I don't know if I can—"

"Please," she interrupted, her voice cracking. She stepped closer, her hands reaching out but stopping just short of touching me, as if she was afraid I might pull away. "Please, Stephanie. I'll tell you everything. I'll be completely honest. Just . . . don't walk away from me. Not yet. I can't lose you without trying to make things right."

I stood there, my mind racing and my heart torn between the anger and pain that still lingered. Not to mention the undeniable pull I felt toward her. I could see the sincerity in her eyes, the fear of losing me etched into her every feature. The woman standing before me wasn't the confident, assured Ashlyn I had first met. This was someone who had been stripped down to her core, someone who was genuinely afraid of what the future might hold without me in it.

Silence stretched between us, thick and heavy, filled with all the unspoken words, the hurt, and the love that had once been so strong. I wanted to protect myself, to turn away and preserve whatever was

left of my shattered heart. But I also knew that if I walked away now, if I didn't at least hear her out,

I might regret it for the rest of my life.

Taking a deep breath, I finally met her gaze. "Okay," I said softly, the word escaping before I had

time to reconsider. "Okay, Ashlyn. I'll listen. But I need you to be honest with me. Completely honest."

A look of relief washed over her face, her shoulders sagging slightly as if a heavy burden had just been lifted. "I will," she promised, her voice firm despite the tears glistening in her eyes. "I'll tell you everything, Stephanie. I just need you to know how much I care about you, how much I've always cared."

I nodded, the tension in my chest easing just a fraction. "Then let's talk," I said, my voice steadier now. "But not here. Let's go somewhere quiet."

She nodded quickly, her relief palpable, and together we walked back toward the house, the silence between us now less about the distance and more about the tentative hope that maybe—

just maybe—we could begin to mend what had been broken. But as much as I wanted to believe that things could be fixed, I knew that the road ahead would be difficult, filled with hard truths and even harder choices. Still, for the first time in weeks, I allowed myself to hope.

26

ASHLYN

The warm evening air wrapped around us as we walked up the hill, the sky painted in hues of orange and pink as the sun dipped below the horizon. The fields stretched out before us, a vast expanse of green that seemed to go on forever, untouched by the world's chaos. It was quiet here, with just the two of us, with only the gentle rustle of the grass and the occasional chirp of crickets to keep us company. This was where I had always felt most at peace, but tonight, there was a storm brewing inside me, and I knew it was time to face it.

Stephanie walked beside me, her silence heavy with anticipation. I could feel the tension in her, in the way she was bracing herself for whatever I was about to say. My heart ached knowing that I had

caused this, that I had been the one to bring this pain into her life. But if there was any chance of fixing things, I had to be honest. Completely, brutally honest.

When we reached the top of the hill, I stopped, turning to face her. The fading light cast a soft glow over her features, and for a moment, I just looked at her, taking in the woman who had become my

entire world. She was strong, resilient, and beautiful in a way that went way beyond physical appearance.

And I had nearly destroyed everything because of my past.

"Stephanie," I began, my voice trembling slightly as I tried to find the right words. "I don't even know where to start. I've never been good at this—at opening up, at being vulnerable. But I owe you the truth. You deserve that much."

She didn't say anything, just nodded, her eyes fixed on mine, urging me to continue.

"I've always been a player," I said, the words tasting bitter on my tongue. "I never really understood love, not the way other people did. For me, it was always just about the horses. They were the only thing I cared about, the only thing that ever made sense to me. People . . . people were just there. And women- well, they were fun, but never anything more."

I paused, taking a deep breath, the memories of my past flickering through my mind like ghosts.

"And then there was Monica. She was different —rich, powerful, exciting. She was married, so I didn't have to worry about hurting her, about getting too close. To me, it was just sex. A game. I

didn't think about the consequences, about what it might do to her or to me."

Stephanie's gaze never wavered, and I could see the hurt in her eyes, the way my words were cutting into her. But she didn't look away, didn't turn her back on me, and that gave me the strength to keep going.

"Things were good for a while," I continued, my voice growing steadier as I spoke. "But then Monica started to get reckless. She wasn't content with just sneaking around anymore—she wanted more. She wanted me, completely, and she didn't care who knew. We were nearly caught a few times, and that's when I realized that I couldn't keep going. My career was on the line, and I wasn't going to risk everything I'd worked for because of some fling."

I saw Stephanie flinch at the word "fling," and I cursed myself for how carelessly I'd spoken. But it was the truth, and she needed to hear it. "So I ended it," I said softly. "I thought that would be the end of it, that Monica would move on, and I could go back to focusing on my work. But I underestimated her. Ending things didn't just hurt her—it enraged her. She was used to getting what she wanted, and when I walked away, it wasn't just her heart that was bruised. It was her pride."

I felt the anger rising in me as I remembered how everything had spiraled out of control. "Monica wasn't going to let me go that easily. She made it her mission to ruin me, to make sure I could never work in Kentucky again. She had connections and influence, and she used them to back me into a corner. I had no choice but to sign that stupid agreement, to leave everything I knew behind."

I saw Stephanie's face soften slightly, a glimmer of understanding in her eyes, but I knew the hardest part was still to come. "And then I found you," I whispered, my voice breaking. "I found this ranch, Phantom . . . and I found you. For the first time in my life, I understood what it meant to love. You changed everything, Stephanie. You made me want to be better, to be someone who deserved you."

The tears that had been threatening to fall finally spilled over, and I didn't try to stop them. "I fell in love with you, with this place, with the simple, beautiful life we were building together. I should have

told you the truth from the beginning, but I was scared. Scared that you'd see me for who I really was, that you'd leave me before I had a chance to prove that I could be different, that I could be

better."

I took a shaky breath, wiping at my eyes, trying to regain some composure. "But everything I felt for you was real, Stephanie. It still is. And I know I've hurt you, that I've made you question everything

we had, but I'm begging you—please, give me a chance to make it right. I want to be the woman you deserve, the woman who stands by your side through everything. Just . . . please, give me that chance."

The silence that followed was suffocating, the weight of my confession hanging in the air between us. I could see the conflict in Stephanie's eyes, the way she was grappling with the truth I had just laid bare. Part of me wanted to take it all back, to erase the hurt I had caused, but I knew it was too late for that. All I could do now was wait, hope, and pray that she could find it in her heart to forgive me.

I watched as she turned her gaze out toward the fields, her face bathed in the warm glow of the setting sun. I could see the tears welling in her eyes, the way her shoulders trembled as she fought

to keep her emotions in check. And all I wanted was to hold her, to comfort her, but I knew this was her moment, her decision to make.

"And," I added. "There is something else, I have money, Stephanie. I have enough money that I can help with the ranch. We can make it something special together. I didn't tell you that, either. I didn't want you to think I was trying to buy you, but here it is, the whole truth."

Finally, after what felt like an eternity, Stephanie turned back to me, her eyes filled with a mixture of pain, love, and something else—something that looked like hope.

"Ashlyn…" she began, her voice trembling, and I felt my heart stop as I waited for her next words. "I've missed you so much."

"I'd like us to try again. Try and make things work. I am sorry for refusing to let you explain. Just what you did, not being honest with me. It just took me right back to what happened with Sophia. I know the situation was different and you aren't with Monica. But, it just felt so the same. Like I thought I knew you so well, and yet there you were hiding so much of yourself, of your past and of something that was infiltrating your present."

She sighed deeply and took my hand and squeezed it. "Is that everything?" she asked, earnestly. "The whole truth?"

I nodded and I hated myself for causing the pain I saw in her blue eyes.

"Sit down," she said and she sat on the grass of the hillside overlooking the ranch. I sat quietly next to her. "There is something else I need to tell you," she said and I raised my head enquiringly. "You remember I told you about Sophia?" she asked and I nodded in response.

"The woman you loved in the army?"

"Yes," she said.

"The one with the secret husband?" I asked.

"Yes," she said again. "That wasn't the whole story that I gave you." She sighed deeply and looked into the distance with a desolate sadness in her eyes.

She continued, "Sophia told me about her husband one day. Only a few days before we were due to leave the desert and fly home. We were desperate to get home. Back to US soil. There is something about being in the desert too long and seeing some of the things we saw. It messes with you. It fucks you up. We just wanted to be home so much." She took a pause and swallowed.

"Anyway, she told me about her husband and her future and suggested we could still see each other occasionally. Well, I couldn't. I loved her. Like, really loved her. We had been each other's secret long enough because of the rules of the army and I always imagined that the rest of our lives together would make up for that. I wasn't prepared to go on being her secret forever for the sake of this husband that she was choosing over me. So, I ended things between us. And, that, well that tore me apart."

Her voice cracked and I put my hand on her

thigh so she knew I was there. I could see tears beading in her eyes but I didn't want to interrupt her story.

"Anyway. The next day, I was at work, trying my best to hide my tears from everyone, because you don't get to cry about a secret affair that nobody knew about. And we got a message through that the patrol that had gone out that morning had been hit and they were bringing the casualties back. They told me to prep for surgery." Her breathing quickened and I could see the panic rising within her and I knew she was right back there on that day in the desert. She continued, "I knew, deep within me that it was going to be her. And it was. It was her, Sophia, bleeding out on my operating table." Tears started flooding down her face. She cried and cried and cried and fell into my arms and I held her tightly. "She died," Stephanie cried. "I did everything I could to save her, but she died…" Stephanie was sobbing and sobbing and I held her to me as the pain tore through her. My heart broke for her. This was what she had been hiding all along. This was why she left the army. "The blood," she gasped. "I can't forget her blood, so much blood on the white tiles…"

I held her as she folded further into me and came apart in my arms. I rocked her like a baby and I stroked her hair. Eventually she just lay placidly across my lap and closed her eyes. I wondered if she was sleeping, but I don't think she was. I think it had all just been too much to relive so she had shut down.

It was a long time later she came back round and I lifted her up slowly and carefully and she leant on me as we walked slowly back to the house.

∽

I made pasta for us and made a fire and we sat beside it through the evening. We didn't speak further, but there was a closeness between us that hadn't been there before. Now all our ghosts were out of their boxes and the ghosts of Sophia and Monica loomed large around us. We had to make it through that part and wait for them to fade away and leave us. Just us. Ashlyn and Stephanie.

∽

The following day Stephanie rose late. I did the morning chores of the ranch alongside Melody. She never asked about what happened and I didn't tell.

When Stephanie and I were alone in the kitchen, I made coffee and we sat down together.

"I love you, Ashlyn," she said. "I really love you. In a way that terrifies me. I'm terrified you will decide I'm not really the one. I'm also terrified you might die." She took a deep breath. "But, I realize these fears are largely irrational based on what I have been through. And I do feel something with you that is life changing. So, I want us to try and make this work. I want love to be enough this time."

She stood up and looked out at the door.

I smiled and joined her, taking her in my arms as we stood in the wide doorway looking out at the vast open expanse of the ranch in front of us. Horses grazed happily. I looked at Phantom as he flicked his beautiful black tail to ward off a fly.

"I'd like that too. I know my own issues, my own past has shaped my behaviours. But, I love you more than anything. I want to be a better person for you. I've been happy and at peace when I've been with you, here in this magical place and I want to be again. I think we can have our happy ever after, you know. And, I think we deserve it."

She nuzzled into my shoulder and pulled my arms tighter around her.

I rocked her in my arms as we stared out at our future.

EPILOGUE
STEPHANIE

The path to forever is never smooth. It took weeks, months, and even years to navigate the tangled mess of legalities surrounding Ashlyn's contract. The fight was grueling, filled with endless paperwork, court battles, and sleepless nights where the fear of losing everything loomed over us like a storm cloud. But through it all, we stood by each other, determined to carve out a future that belonged to us, not dictated by the mistakes and the traumas of the past.

Telling Ashlyn about what happened with Sophia was the first time I had spoken to anyone about it. And it was the first time I had cried in front of anyone. The first time I had ever told the truth, the whole truth and falling apart in her arms had been a balm on the open wound of my trauma.

But, more was needed. The second person I spoke to was a therapist, Tracey, I told her everything over hours of sessions. All the traumas and losses I had been through during my time in the Army culminating in Sophia's betrayal and then ultimately her death. And, I cried and cried and cried for hours in her comforting presence. I wouldn't say I was healed. There is no healed for the level of trauma I had been through, but I was finding a way through it all with Ashlyn by my side.

And it felt ok to let Sophia Clark out of the box in my head more and more. Sometimes when she would flick into my mind, some memory of her, I would share it with Ashlyn. And she cared. Ashlyn has cared so very much for me right from the start.

And, Ashlyn would talk about Monica sometimes and I would listen. We had both been betrayed by women we had trusted, so we had common ground there. She saw a therapist, too. She worked on her commitment issues, and why she always ran away when things got hard.

I do sometimes fear Ashlyn dying. I have

spoken to Tracey about that quite a lot. There is no answer for that. Death will come for us all sooner or later and I need to make my peace with that. Losing Sophia to death was so tightly tangled up with losing her to her betrayal and it has been hard to move past that.

The one thing I don't doubt is Ashlyn's commitment to me and to the horses and our home.

∼

We fostered two children. Amy and Christy, sisters aged 12 and 14 who had been through a lot of trauma in their short lives. We will offer long term sanctuary to them. It hasn't been easy, we all have our own personal darkness, but we love them so dearly.

It feels good being able to give to them and though we can't make everything ok for them, we see progress in them every day in long summer days on the ranch with the horses. Oh, how they love the horses.

We got a dog too. A big rangy Belgian Malinois called Max- a retired bomb detection dog who made his way to the ranch from one of my army contacts. He finished his service early due to injury, but he has gone through his rehab on the ranch and he will live out the rest of his days in peace with us here.

∼

Bill, with his deep love for horses and unwavering belief in us, became an invaluable ally. He worked tirelessly to help us sort out the financial mess that had threatened to bury the ranch. He found creative solutions, negotiated with the bank, and slowly but surely, we began to see the light at the end of the tunnel. The ranch, our sanctuary, was safe.

Melody, too, found her own path to happiness. It was at one of the events, a modest local horse show where we were showing off Phantom's progress, that she met him. A quiet man with kind eyes who seemed afraid of his own shadow, but whom, to everyone's surprise, effortlessly slipped into life on the ranch as though he had always been meant to be there. Their relationship blossomed in the same way Melody had on the ranch —slowly, naturally, without any pressure to be anything other than what it was. And as they grew closer, it became clear that the two of them had found something special, something rare and precious.

The four of us—Stephanie, Ashlyn, Melody, and her quiet man—poured our time, heart, and soul into the ranch. It became more than just a place to live; it became a refuge, a place of healing and

growth. More and more horses came to us, each one with a story and a past that had left its own marks. We took them in, cared for them, trained them, and watched as they transformed, their spirits slowly mending under the love and attention we gave them.

And it wasn't just horses who found solace on the ranch. People began to come too—some to train, others to learn, and many just to volunteer. They came from all walks of life- a lot of ex army- each with their own burdens, their own demons to face. We made some of the houses on the ranch into boarding houses and we welcomed people in. We built our own community out here under the vast texan skies. The ranch became an escape for them, a place where they could find solace from whatever life had thrown at them.

Time rolled by and the ranch flourished. What

had once been a small, struggling farm became a thriving community. We built new stables, expanded the pastures, and even added another guest house for those who needed a place to stay. The land, once wild and untamed, became a symbol of resilience and hope.

~

Phantom, the horse who had brought us all together, became a legend in his own right. He never raced in Kentucky, but he didn't need to. His strength, his spirit, and the bond he shared with Ashlyn became the stuff of local lore. People came from miles around just to see him, to watch him run, and to witness the connection between horse and rider that had defied all the odds.

Ashlyn competed him in races, but then also we retrained him for the rodeo- for Barrel Racing which he was very good at. She also trained him the English way and moved onto Dressage and Eventing with him. Phantom was that kind of horse- the talent to do anything.

~

As for us, the years softened the edges of our pasts. The pain, the mistakes, and the regrets—they didn't disappear, but they no longer defined us. We learned to forgive, to let go, and to embrace the love that had grown between us. It wasn't always easy—nothing worth having ever is—but we learned to navigate the rough patches. To hold on to each other when the storms threatened to pull us apart.

Our wedding day was my fondest memory. We stood together on the ranch, with Amy, Christy and Max at our sides, ready to declare our love in front of the people who mattered most to us. We called it a service of love and union, a celebration not just of our commitment to each other, but of everything we had overcome to be there. The sun bathed the ranch in a warm, golden light, the fields were a vibrant green, and the air was filled with the scent of wildflowers and fresh hay. It was perfect, in every way that mattered.

As I stood there, looking at Ashlyn with the ranch as our backdrop, I felt a rush of emotion that nearly took my breath away. We had been through so much together—heartache, challenges, moments of doubt—but in that moment, all of it seemed worth it. Ashlyn was everything I had ever wanted and more, and I knew with absolute certainty that this was where I was meant to be.

We could argue until the sun came up about the best way to break in a horse—our stubbornness clashing like thunder—but all it took was one look from her, and my heart would skip a beat. The butterflies in my stomach had never left. Their wings might have softened with time, but they were always there, fluttering gently whenever she was near. I'd feel them when the sunrise would catch Ashlyn's face as she dismounted from a ride, her skin glowing in the early morning light and her expression one of peace and contentment. I'd feel them when her laughter filled the room, the sound warm and familiar—especially when she found herself caught up in a rerun of *Friends*.

And every time her fingers unexpectedly brushed against my bare skin, whether in a gentle caress or a playful touch, the butterflies would take flight, reminding me of the love that had only grown

deeper with time. It was during those small, quiet moments that I realized just how much she meant to me—how much we had built together, and how far we had come.

Our life together wasn't perfect, but it was ours. We had our disagreements and our struggles, but we always found our way back to each other. The ranch had become a part of us, a reflection of the

love and dedication we had poured into it. As we exchanged our vows, I knew we were ready for whatever the future might hold.

The service of love and union was more than just a wedding; it was a celebration of everything we had fought for and everything we had become. As we stood there, hand in hand, surrounded by the people who had supported us, I felt an overwhelming sense of gratitude. The path to forever had been rough and winding, but it had led us here, to this moment, and I wouldn't have wanted it any other way.

Ashlyn was my partner, my love, my home. Every time I looked at her—whether in the glow of the sunrise, the warmth of the evening, or the quiet moments we shared—I knew I had found something rare and precious. Something worth fighting for and holding on to, for the rest of my life. And as we walked back down the aisle, surrounded by the cheers and laughter of our friends and family, I knew that no matter the challenges that lay ahead, we would face them together, with love as our guide.

Through it all, we never forgot the lessons we had learned. That love is not always simple. That it takes work, patience, and a willingness to fight for what truly matters. That trust, once broken, can be rebuilt—but only if both people are willing to put in the effort. And that sometimes, the most beautiful things in life come from the most unexpected places.

The ranch stood as a testament to that truth—a place where broken things could be mended, and where lost souls could find their way home. As the sun set each evening, casting its golden light over the fields, we would stand together, knowing that whatever the future held, we would face it together, as a family. The path to forever might be rough and winding, but it was ours, and we wouldn't have had it any other way.

∽

The evening had settled into a quiet calm, the kind of stillness that only the ranch could offer. The air was warm, with the scent of earth and hay lingering as the last light of the sun dipped below the

horizon. Inside the house, the only sound that could be heard was the soft crackle of the fire in the hearth. It cast a gentle glow across the room. This was one of those rare moments when everything felt perfectly in place and I found myself drawn to Ashlyn, who was sitting on the couch, her legs curled up beneath her, lost in thought. She looked up as I entered the room, her eyes catching the light from the fire. For a moment, I just stood there, taking her in. There was something about the way the flickering light played over her features that made my heart skip a beat—a feeling that had never faded, no matter how much time had passed. I moved toward her, my steps slow and deliberate, as if I were savoring every inch of space between us.

When I reached her, I didn't say a word. Instead, I gently cupped her face in my hands, my fingers tracing the line of her jaw, feeling the warmth of her skin beneath my touch. She looked up at me with those green eyes, so full of emotion, and I felt a familiar flutter in my chest, the kind that always preceded a kiss. And then, without hesitation, I leaned in and pressed my lips to hers.

The kiss was soft at first, a tentative brush of lips that sent a shiver down my spine. But as the seconds passed, it deepened, and the warmth between us grew. Pulling me closer to her. Her hands found their way to my waist and I felt her fingers curl into the fabric of my shirt, holding me to her as if she couldn't bear to let go. I let out a soft sigh against her lips, my body responding instinctively to the closeness. The heat building between us.

I could feel her breath quicken as I tilted my head, deepening the kiss—our mouths moving in a rhythm that was as old as time itself. My hands slipped from her face to her shoulders, then down her arms. Tracing the contours of her body with a reverence that came from knowing every inch of her intimately. She was warm and soft beneath my touch, her skin like silk as I let my hands explore the familiar territory.

Ashlyn responded with a hunger that matched my own, her hands sliding up my back, pulling me even closer until there was no space left between us. Our kiss grew more urgent, more demanding, and I felt the fire inside me ignite, my need for her overwhelming. I could feel every beat of my heart, every breath she took as our bodies pressed together. The intensity of the moment drowning out everything else.

I pulled back just enough to look into her eyes, and the sight of her—lips slightly parted, cheeks flushed, eyes dark with desire—sent another wave of heat coursing through me. Without a word, I

leaned in again, my lips finding the curve of her neck, trailing soft kisses along her skin, feeling the way she trembled beneath my touch. Her hands were in my hair now, her fingers tangling in the

strands as she tilted her head back, giving me more access.

"Stephanie," she whispered, her voice breathless, filled with a need that mirrored my own. The sound of my name on her lips, spoken in that tone, was all the encouragement I needed. I let my hands roam, sliding beneath the fabric of her shirt, feeling the warmth of her skin against my palms. She arched into my touch, her breath hitching as I found the sensitive spots that I knew so well. My fingers traced the lines of her body, memorizing every dip, every curve, as if it were the

first time.

Her hands moved too, exploring me with the same intensity, the same desire. There was a sense of urgency between us, a need to be as close as possible, to erase any distance that might have existed. I could feel her heartbeat against my chest, fast and steady, matching the rhythm of my own.

As we moved together, the room seemed to fade away, leaving only the two of us, lost in each other. Every touch, every kiss, was a reminder of the connection we shared—a connection that had

only deepened over time. The world outside might have been uncertain, filled with challenges and doubts, but here, in this moment, everything was clear. I pushed her gently back onto the couch, leaning over her, my hands framing her face as I kissed

her again, long and slow. Savoring the taste of her, the feel of her beneath me. She responded with a soft moan, her hands sliding down to my hips, pulling me closer. The sound of her, the way she

moved against me, sent a thrill through my entire body. I couldn't help but smile against her lips.

I pulled back slightly, just enough to look at her. The sight of her lying there, hair spread out like a dark halo, eyes half-closed with desire, was almost too much to bear. I leaned in, my lips brushing against hers as I whispered, "I love you, Ashlyn."

Her eyes opened fully at my words, and for a moment, she just looked at me, her expression softening, filled with a tenderness that made my heart swell. "I love you too, Stephanie," she replied, her voice filled with the same depth of emotion.

And then we were kissing again, and the rest of the world fell away. There was only us, only this moment, filled with the kind of intimacy that came from knowing and loving someone so completely. Our bodies moved together in a dance as old as time. Each touch, each kiss, became a testament to the love we had built, to the life we had created together.

In that moment, nothing else mattered. There was no past and no future—only the here and now, and the love that filled the space between us. It was a love that had been tested, a love that had grown

stronger with each challenge. As we lay there, wrapped up in each other, I knew this was where I was meant to be. With her, always.

FREE BOOK

Pick up my book, Summer Love for FREE when you sign up to my mailing list.

On a beach in France, Summer crashes into Max's life and changes everything. This is a hot and heady summer romance. https://BookHip.com/MFPGZAX

My mailing list is the best place to be the first to find out about new releases, Free books, special offers and price drops. You'll also find out a bit about my life and the inspiration behind the stories and the characters. Oh, and you'll love Summer Love. :)

ALSO BY MARGAUX FOX

Check out the next book in the Infinite Tenderness Series at the following link!

mybook.to/IT5

Have you read my Her Royal Bodyguard Series?

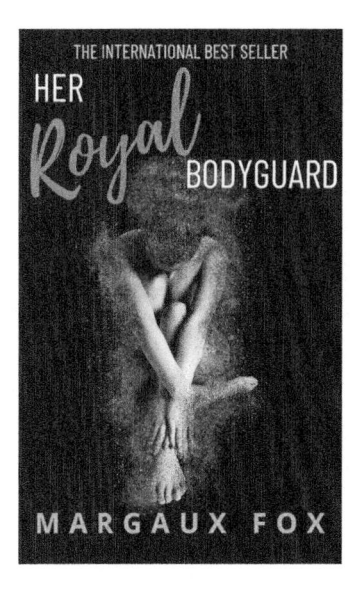

getbook.at/HRB

Printed in Great Britain
by Amazon